LEND ME YOUR EARS

LEND ME YOUR EARS

AARON MARC STEIN

PUBLISHED FOR THE CRIME CLUB BY

DOUBLEDAY & COMPANY, INC.

GARDEN CITY, NEW YORK

1976

All of the characters in this book
are fictitious, and any resemblance
to actual persons, living or dead,
is purely coincidental.

ISBN 0-385-12245-4
Library of Congress Catalog Card Number 76–18368
Copyright © 1976 by Aaron Marc Stein
All Rights Reserved
Printed in the United States of America
First Edition

For
Peter Poor
Beaujolais
Barbara Fontneau
and
Nelson F. Harpsichords
with the
love and gratitude
of the
author

LEND ME YOUR EARS

I.

Italy is the home of my heart, and if you should happen to be one of those lugs who say Italy would be all right if it didn't have the Italians in it, you could be running head on into a knock-down and drag-out argument with Matt Erridge. That's who's talking: Matthew Erridge, American, Italy-lover, engineer, and a triple-plated, trouble-prone guy.

I don't go looking for it. Maybe that's because I'm an amiable live-and-let-live, love-and-let-love type, or maybe it's only because I don't have to: I can just sit tight and wait for trouble to come looking for me. It never misses. It always knows where to find me.

Since the work I do takes me to all the near and most of the far places of the world, finding me isn't always easy, but grief knows the way. So, if I tell you that even trouble is better in Italy, that there is something special about having it hit you when you have Italians around you, I know whereof I speak. I've known trouble in many places. I'm equipped to make comparisons.

What I'm telling you about happened at a time when I wasn't working. I had a noodle of time between jobs, and since Italy happened to be handy, I headed for it. I'd heard the horror stories—the postmen were on strike, nobody was getting any mail, bills were being delivered by messenger, but nobody was bothering to send messengers to pay them.

If you have a bit of leisure time, where better to be than a place where nobody can get at you with importunate letters or even with those juicy offers no sane man can let himself refuse? There would be the telephone, of course, but do you know the Italian telephone? There's a slender reed.

The postal strike was only part of it. There was kidnapping. The word was out that throughout the peninsula and its associated islands kidnapping had developed into a major growth industry. I gave it little thought. It's been a long time since I was a kid and also, the way I saw it, when crime gets to be big business, it can't avoid falling into the trap of Harvard Business School methods. You know. Cost analysis. Cost-profit ratios. All that jazz.

Assessing Matt Erridge as a kidnappee, I couldn't make it that he assessed for much. I'm not rich enough. I'm not that well connected. Also, I'm just that much more-than-average competent in the self-defense department to deter any big operator, who will be prone to weigh risk and effort against potential profit.

So what's so great about Italy? There are the obvious things like the food, the wine, the beauty, and all that art. All over the place, of course, art is getting kidnapped maybe as much as people, but there's so much of it that you could use a couple of lifetimes if you wanted to go around looking at what's left.

And there are the people. More than anyone, Italians know how to live. They've got themselves a country where nothing ever works, but they live in it and they live with it and the way they do their living makes what the rest of us do seem no better than merely existing.

Italians take nothing calmly, but they know how to take everything. They're the world's great connoisseurs of chaos. I think they'd get bored if they lived in a well-ordered world. If they can't laugh, they cry. If they can't complain, they rejoice. They like noise and confusion, and they are great at making both. They enjoy everything. They take nothing lying down. They roll with the punches and life goes on.

It started in Naples and it started with a girl. She wasn't an Italian girl. She was American and she was beautiful in what always has seemed to me to be a special American way. Long, suntanned legs with just enough muscle on them to give them shape and to tell you she'd be okay on a tennis court. Cool, gray eyes that, even if they handed you no more than a glance, were a sure bet to step up your heart beat. Lips that didn't look as though they'd been made for kissing but did look as though they could be taught, and that's the best way for lips to look. I'm a firm believer in education.

I needn't go on.

I've been told I have a bad habit and, if I would only break myself of it, I could keep out of trouble. The habit under fire, of course, is looking at girls, so it's no good talking about it. That kind of advice is as good as telling a man to stop getting hungry or suggesting to him that he give up breathing.

Anyhow it's a crock. I can look back over the troubles I've seen and I can't deny that girl watching got me into a lot of them, but not nearly all. I've been in places so far removed from all the amenities—and those, of course, include girls—and even in places like that trouble has come and found me. So it's only part of the time that the girls bring the trouble. At least as often the trouble brings them, and I don't want to recall the times when there was no girl at all and Erridge had to take his trouble neat.

So it started with a girl, which is understandable; but it also started in a bank, which may be less understandable. It's not that anyone is going to argue that trouble and banks are inseparable, but girl trouble?

The bank was in the Via Santa Lucia, which is about as tourist-stuffed a street as you're likely to find anywhere. That, of course, makes it a bank that sees American girls almost as often as it sees money. This one, however, wasn't just another American tourist. From the way every eye was on her you could know that they didn't often see a girl that lovely.

She shoved a check across the counter and in due course a stack of lira notes was shoved back at her but only after the check had been subjected to the scrutiny of every employee from the porter, who was oil-mopping the floor tiles to eliminate footprints and leave the floor slick enough to promote damage suits, all the way up to the big-wheel type in the striped pants, morning coat, and the gold cuff links that looked to have so much heft to them that it could have been that they represented the bank's total assets. He couldn't have been anything so insignificant as the manager. He would need to have been the bank president at least, though I was guessing Italy's Minister of Finance specially flown down from Rome to goggle at the American peachcake's check.

If there was anyone in that bank who was so much the insensate clod that the girl's looks hadn't moved him, her lira notes did it. It's not too often that most people get to see a stack of banknotes attain that much altitude. Everyone seemed to be impressed—everyone, that is, except Ms. Moneybags herself.

She never bothered even to glance at the receipt slip. She

didn't stop to count the money before she stuffed it in her purse. It seemed careless, but you had to recognize that making a count would have taken a little time and she maybe had better things to do. The exchange, of course, being what it is, you do get lira in a much higher stack than you would have in the dollar equivalent, but in any language she was picking up what would be an impressive stack of bread.

She just dropped it into her handbag and started for the street. The handbag was one of those fiber deals from mainland China, and by the look of them you could guess that back there they were used for carrying the bean sprouts and the water chestnuts home from the market, but, in the States, they were the big thing with the chicks who never carried anything home from the market. Maybe it's fun playing like you're a Chinese coolie as long as there's never a chance you'll be one.

She left the bank in a crowd of people, and I was one of the crowd. I had the Porsche parked out front, and for a moment I was tempted just to let Baby sit there a while. What was leading me into temptation, need I tell you, was that long-stemmed American Beauty.

Coming out of the bank, she started down Santa Lucia toward the bay. Down there she was a cinch to turn right along the Via Partenope. Partenope has her kind of hotel. It also has the shops where the view of the bay just might lull you into taking in stride the wildly elevated prices.

My problem was that she could turn right at the bottom of Santa Lucia and stroll along Partenope. I could turn right down there and stroll the way she went, but Baby could never make it. Partenope is one-way and, of course, the wrong way.

I hesitated but it was only for a moment because just then, I did notice something else. I probably noticed it only

because it was so close to her. Let's face it, it was where Erridge would have liked to have been.

It was a kid, maybe fifteen or sixteen. With Neapolitan men it's hard to tell. They play the aging game both ways. They seem to grow up at birth and, maybe because they do it that early, they don't do it all the way. Little boys in Naples are hardened cynics. Grown men are carefree little boys. Maybe that doesn't go for all Neapolitans, but it does go for the street types and what was cuddling up close to her was street type of purest ray serene.

As we came out to Santa Lucia, the eye which he should by all reasonable expectations have had for nobody but her, flicked away for a moment. It flicked to his counterpart who was waiting at the curb astride a motorcycle. A signal passed. The motorcyclist kicked his engine to life and waited. I could smell what was coming and it made up my mind for me. I jumped for the Porsche. True enough, Baby couldn't make the turn into Partenope, but no more could the motorcycle.

She was playing right into their hands, setting herself up. Santa Lucia is no back alley. It's a wide street with amply wide sidewalks. With all that sidewalk, she was using only the edge of it that ran along the curb, and she had her Chinese straw carryall slung from her curbside shoulder.

The kid left her side and jumped aboard the motorcycle, joining his pal. They waited for maybe a ten count before they took off after her. If you're a man who can get a kick out of watching a consummate craftsman, you should have been there. The timing, the co-ordination, the sure touch, those kids had the lot.

The motorcycle roared past her and the kid who was riding in back had to have had years of practice on carousels. It couldn't have been smoother or more efficient. He just reached out, got a good grip on the shoulder strap, and

hung on. He didn't even have to yank it free. The motorcycle supplied the power. The strap parted, and the motorcycle roared off toward the bay.

As I gunned Baby after it, I was able to catch out of the corner of my eye only a momentary glimpse of the girl. She was just standing there with her mouth hanging open looking stunned. It was the look of a pole-axed steer, and you're not going to believe this, Charlie, but on her even that looked good.

The motorcycle driver had his wheels going all out, but all out for a motorcycle is no more than a walk for a Porsche. On any open road Baby and I could have been on them within the first hundred feet, but in the heart of Naples open roads are what you haven't got. Those kids went weaving through the traffic like a buttered eel.

The best I could do was keep them in sight, but the best they could do was keep a short lead on me, and even for that they had to go in for so much circus stuff that even the passenger didn't have a free hand. The standard procedure calls for doing a quick job of fishing money and other valuables out of the bag, stowing loot in pockets, and flinging bag away. With one hand needed for hanging on to the motorcycle, however, and the other needed for hanging on to the bag, my young purse snatcher was finding himself clean out of hands.

As long as they kept to the heavily traveled streets, it was a stalemate. They couldn't work loose from me and I couldn't come down on them. For them it was just wild evasive action and hang on tight. For me it was hang in as close as I could manage and keep the pressure on.

For a time, while they were leading me a chase through Chiatamone and then down to the bay by the Piazza Vittoria, it looked as though this could go on forever, except that I knew that it wouldn't. Baby holds a lot more fuel than any motorcycle, and sooner or later they had to run out of gas. That was if they could carry on that long. The odds were it was going to be quicker than that. Slithering through all those narrow places in the roaring traffic, they were bound sooner or later to head into a hole that would no longer be there when they got to it. Then there would be a couple of dead kids splattered over the pavement.

I didn't want it to go that way. What the hell, it's been a good piece of time now since purse snatching was a capital offense. All I was after was the recovery of the bread and baubles and maybe knocking a couple of young curly heads together.

As soon as they made the turn through Vittoria to head for the bay, I could read them. They were out to do the left that would take them into Partenope there at the far end of it. Then it would be zipping along the bay front, Partenope, Nazario Sauro, and then cut back inland through the wild traffic that churns between the Royal Palace and the Piazza del Plebiscito and off into the Via Roma. Somewhere along Roma it would be the quick turn into one of the side streets where either they would disappear into one of a dozen tenements or else they would turn and meet me, but with an army of street buddies at their back.

That, of course, would be what they were aiming for even though the chances of their making it that far before they ran afoul of the police would be of the slimmest. Even in Naples there is a limit to the official toleration of insanity on wheels.

All the same it was going to be more to my liking if I could get them headed the other way where there would be less chance that they would kill themselves and less possibility of intervention. I might as well admit it. I was almost half on their side. I like technique and they were showing me great technique. Also, since everything about the lady indicated that there would be plenty more where that had come from, I was ready to call this loss something less than she deserved. I can't pretend that I was without motive. Coming to the aid of a maiden in distress can be a great way of getting to know the maiden.

Catching a break in the traffic, I zoomed in and cut them off from the left. For a moment it looked as though the chase might end right there, but they also caught a break in the traffic and veered away from me. I was satisfied to settle for that. I now had them headed the way I wanted them to go.

I was chasing them along the bay front on the Via Caracciolo. Down there past Vittoria the name changes from Partenope to Caracciolo, and Caracciolo takes two-way traffic. We were now headed away from the thickest traffic areas, and my chances for heading them in the directions I wanted were improving all the time. All it was going to take now would be to block them off from the one turn that would give them access to the vehicular tunnels that run under the Posillipo high ground where it overlooks the bay from the north.

Once I would have them past that, they would be committed to the hairpin turns of the switchbacks that carry you up the Posillipo hill. If you don't know Naples, Posillipo is a residential area and conspicuously upper-upper middle. There's a lot of new construction up there, so it gets the people who want central heating, modern plumbing, all the twentieth-century comfort gadgets plus that famous view of the Bay of Naples. They are, of course, also the people who are able to pay for it.

Traffic is never too heavy up there, and in the middle of a midweek morning when the men are in their offices and only the women are likely to be on wheels, it's pleasantly sparse. On those reasonably deserted switchbacks the

Porsche was going to give me every advantage. The roads would be clear enough to give me the good of her extra speed. Also, she has the maneuverability that was going to let me do the things that must send any motorcycle tail over teakettle.

Zipping the Porsche in between them and the turnoff Caracciolo, I kept it hanging to the left of them, holding them out of the Via Mergellina and forcing them into the right turn that committed them to the switchback climb. Once they'd made the turn, I had them where I wanted them. A motorcycle has to put out all it's got to make the climb. For Baby it's a breeze.

Also, having the road to ourselves, I could close in on them tight. We were heading into a series of quick, U-turn curves and it was going to be a matter of how gutsy the driver was going to be in negotiating them with the hot breath of the Porsche on his neck. He had come up with plenty of nerve while he was threading through the traffic down below, but I had him figured for a city body for whom slithering through Neapolitan traffic would be bred in the bone. We were about to see how well he could do when he had to make like a mountain goat.

He didn't do well. He managed the first bend but only at an angle that had to scare the pants off him. Coming into the second turn, he gave up. He pulled over to the side and they waited for me to make my move. I swung the Porsche around, pocketing them against a tall garden wall. If they tried to take off on foot, they were going to have to come past Baby either at her nose or her tail.

They weren't about to risk any of that. They waited for me with their backs against that wall, but it wasn't surrender. It was everything else but, Charlie. I was coming up against two knives, and from the way they looked, they knew how to use them.

If it had been just one of them, I'd have gone for the knife; but two knives can run a man uncomfortably close to the borders of Superman country.

It can be done but you have to be prepared to get at least moderately cut up in the process and, if you want to play it for a guarantee of any kind against anything more than moderate, you can't go into it holding anything back. The first one of them you hit you have to hit hard enough so he'll be dumped right out of the action and he'll stay dumped long enough to let you get everything under complete control.

If that was the way it had to be, that was the way it had to be, but I wasn't so hungry for it that I didn't want to try something else first. Maybe it didn't need to be that rough either on me or on them.

I only half started out of the Porsche and I came with my hand in my jacket pocket. I carry a pipe in that pocket and my hand found it. It was positioned right for what I had in mind, mouthpiece end forward. Aiming it in their direction under pocket cover, I found a good assortment of Neapolitan gutter words and sprinkled them around the command I snarled.

Just catch me on any of the TV reruns of the old gangster movies. I was Eddie Robinson. I was Jimmy Cagney. I was the hijacker heisting the truckload of booze in cool defiance of the full power of the mob.

"Drop them."

(The surrounding words defy translation.)

They looked at me. They looked at my threatening pocket. They looked at their knives. They looked at each other. They sighed. They shrugged. The knives clattered to the pavement.

"Now pitch me the bag."

This time they didn't sigh and they didn't shrug. They

just looked at me, at my threatening pocket, and at each other.

"We'll make a deal," the purse snatcher suggested.

The driver made it more specific.

"A three-way split."

"No deal. Just pitch it over."

"Fifty-fifty."

"No deal. The whole thing."

"That's not reasonable," the purse snatcher protested.

"I'm out all the gas you made me use up," the driver complained.

"That's business," I said. "There's the days you make a profit. There's the days you take a loss. This is one of your loss days. So you used up gas. You're making me use up time."

"It isn't fair," the purse snatcher said.

I filled them in on the facts of life.

"We can't go on hanging around here this way," I told them. "Any minute now we'll have the *carabinieri* coming by. Up around here, where the rich people live, they have plenty of protection. They come along and find us like this, I'll have to tell them that you are thieves. So then they'll have the bag and they'll have you. I'll have nothing for the gas and the time you made me use. So it will be one of my loss days, but I'll have my freedom. Since there's no way you can win, is it worth it to you to sit in jail just so I can be a loser too? Be reasonable. Don't you want to get back down to Santa Lucia before the banks close? You can't do yourself any good up here."

Sighing again, the purse snatcher made a move toward the bag. The driver grabbed at his arm. He wasn't quite through bargaining.

"You take this one," he said. "You leave us alone on our next one?"

He was asking for a promise. I gave him half a one. I had a feeling that it would sound more in character that way, and anyhow I wasn't prepared to hand them any unconditional license to steal.

"Just make sure you don't make a play on anything I've got staked out for myself. Don't make that same mistake again."

Now they both sighed.

"You're a hard man," the purse snatcher said.

"And you don't want to find out how hard I can be."

They didn't. He pitched the bag to me.

I put up my left for a one-handed catch. My right couldn't be spared from keeping my pocket on dead aim. Again one-handed, I upended it over the seat beside me and dumped its contents. As far as I could tell, it was all there. The great wad of lira notes, passport, pen, lipstick, handkerchief, checkbook, comb, and perfume atomizer. I tried to think of what else the cookie could have been carrying and I hadn't the first idea. That didn't mean I couldn't make sure.

I ordered them to turn out their pockets. At that they balked.

"You've taken everything we got."

"Turn them out. Anything that's yours I'll let you keep. Anything out of this bag is mine and I want it."

They turned out their pockets. Not much showed that wasn't just pocket. A couple of crumpled packs of Nazionales, matches, some coins, nothing else, not even enough for another pack of cigarettes when the Nazionales would run out.

I peeled a thousand-lira note off the roll, crumpled it into a tight ball, and pitched it to them. A thousand lira? At that time not quite two bucks.

With that I pulled the Porsche out of there. I was

tempted to bring the pipe out of my pocket and clamp the menacing mouthpiece between my teeth as I drove away, but I didn't do it. Sadism has never been my bag and they were young.

They could be having a lot of life ahead of them and I wasn't about to risk shortening it by giving them any dangerous ideas. The day could hit when they would come up against a real gun.

I headed on up toward the top of the grade. I knew that they would be doing a lightning job of pulling themselves together and hightailing it out of there. I also knew that the direction they would be taking would be the other way, down into the flat where the tourists are and the banks and the *cambio* shops.

A couple of switchbacks farther along I pulled in to the curb and stopped to take inventory. I dipped into my billfold for a thousand-lira note and put it with the rest of the horde. Erridge passes out his own largesse. He's not anyone's almoner.

That taken care of, I looked over her stuff. The passport was the obvious good lead. It would tell me her name, and without it, she would have to be over at the American consulate reporting the loss and getting set up for a replacement. If I didn't find her there, they would have to know where she could be found.

I picked the passport up off the seat and an envelope fell out of it. That's the Erridge luck. It was a letter. It gave me everything I needed, her name, her Naples address. The address was what I would have guessed. The Hotel Excelsior. At first sight I had spotted her for the *grande luxe* type, and along Partenope *grande luxe* is the Excelsior or the Vesuvio, with the American tourist more likely to go for the Excelsior.

The name I just couldn't believe. The thing was

addressed to *Signorina* Cuddles Martin. Would you have believed Cuddles, Charlie?

I flipped the passport open. For a moment I almost forgot what I was after. You know passport pictures. Hers, of course, didn't begin to do her justice. Have you ever seen one that did anybody justice? All the same, hers was something to dream over. She was that terrific. I tore myself loose from the picture and checked the name. It was Catherine Martin. I could go with that.

II.

I rolled down to the bay and went straight through into Partenope and along to the Excelsior. Yes, Miss Catherine Martin was registered. Yes, Miss Catherine Martin was in. Yes, they would ring Miss Catherine Martin for the gentleman. No, they wouldn't give the gentleman her room number so that he could ring her on his own. The Excelsior gives its guests better protection than they are ever likely to give themselves. Of guests like Catherine Martin, I was thinking, that had to be the truth.

But then they had her on the phone and I was soon making some quick revisions in my thinking. Cool? She was more than cool. Chilly. The big freeze. Chilled steel.

"Miss Martin?" I said.

"Speaking, but I'd like to know whom I'm speaking to."

"Erridge. Matthew Erridge. I'm nobody you know."

"So why should I be speaking to you then?"

"Okay. You were brought up never to speak to strange men, but you lost your purse this morning."

"I didn't lose it. I never lose anything. It was taken from me, taken by surprise and by force."

"Exactly. I was there. I saw it happen."

"Did you enjoy it?"

"I thought you might want it back."

"Now that's what I call good thinking. Not everyone would have thought of that."

"Not everyone is down in the lobby waiting for you to leave off being smart and snotty if only for just long enough to let me tell you that I have it complete with your passport and your lira and your checkbook and I think all the rest of your bits and pieces, and if you ask nicely, I'll come right up and turn it over to you."

"What was your name again?"

"My name again is Matthew Erridge."

"Very good, Mr. Erridge. Somebody will be down."

I was about to ask her if it would be someone who needed a lesson in manners or someone else, but I was left talking into a dead phone. She'd hung up on me.

There was only one reason why I waited. If she had been only as beautiful and sexy as, let's say, a movie star, I would have hauled myself out of there and gone over to the consulate and dumped her stuff. Let them take her lip when she would come around and condescend to pick it up. They're public servants. I'm not, not public and not private.

But there it was. A spoiled brat, but at least as beautiful as she was spoiled. I was even thinking of all the fun a man might have if he undertook to unspoil her. Do I hear you asking how fatuous can you get? Make it fatheaded.

I didn't have long to wait. He was down within a minute. Before he had even stepped out of the elevator, I knew that he was for me. He had to be a twin brother.

It was just as easy for him. I was the only guy in sight who had a coolie bag with a torn shoulder strap clutched in his hairy fist. I was doing even better than that. I was the only guy there who was carrying any kind of coolie bag.

He came out of the elevator and, spotting me immediately, he took a long pause while he looked me over. It was that appraising look. He could have been deciding whether he wanted to buy me as I stood or call in the experts to determine whether I was sound in wind and limb and free of any hidden dry rot.

But two can play at that game and Erridge was right in there. If he looked like a replica of her, it was as though he'd been done in a tougher material and just roughed in without any of that final polishing to bring all details to their ultimate delicacy.

He was also like her in looking much too rich and in having that air that said, like her, he could also be much too silly and much too arrogant.

It was obvious that he knew I had recognized him. He had the look that much-photographed and heavily publicized celebrities wear. It's the look that says they're accustomed to being recognized, they're braced against its happening again, and they're gearing up to be oh-so-bored by it.

He just stood there, looking at me and waiting for me to come to him. I made no move. I was waiting for Miss Catherine Martin. He was just one more item in the scenery of the Excelsior lobby.

He gave up on it and moved toward me.

"I believe you said the name is Erridge?" he began.

"To you, my boy, I didn't say anything."

"I'm acting for Miss Martin."

"Let me know when you're going into your act. If it happens that I'm still waiting, and if it's a good act, I might watch."

"And what's that supposed to mean?"

"It means that I've taken the time and the trouble to come here to restore Miss Catherine Martin's property to her. Since I was present when Miss Martin lost her property, I'll recognize her when I see her. Also, one of the items I am holding till I can return it to her is her passport. So I can do a positive identification through her passport picture. I've studied the picture and it isn't you. There is a resemblance, but a mere resemblance isn't enough."

"If it's your reward you're worrying about," he said, "I'll take care of that if you haven't already taken care of it yourself out of Miss Martin's money."

"Are you specially hungry for a thick lip, or is it just that you never were taught any manners?"

"You're not satisfied with a reward and no questions asked?"

"That was a question you just asked," I told him.

Turning away from him, I returned to the desk.

"I'll speak to Miss Catherine Martin again," I told the clerk. "Please get me her room."

"That's Mr. Martin you were talking to."

"Mr. Martin is not Miss Martin, or don't you know the difference? If you don't, you're a disgrace to Italy."

Mr. Martin had followed me to the desk. My business with the hotel clerk was being done in Italian, and I could see that Martin was understanding none of it.

I had Catherine on the phone, I went back into English and he got every word.

"Catherine," I said. "Matt Erridge again, or if you like it better, you can call me Petruchio."

"What do you want now?"

"I don't want anything. I assume you will be wanting your stuff back. If you come around to the Hotel Vittoria and ask for me and I'm satisfied with your identification, you will have it. Of course, you may hit the Vittoria when I'm out, but you'll just have to keep coming back till you find me in."

"My brother . . ." she began.

I wasn't waiting for her to finish.

"Your brother isn't you, and it's your property. I'm not turning it over to anyone else."

"He's acting for me."

"So he said. It's not good enough."

"He'll pay you."

"How do I know I can trust him? For that matter, how do I know I can trust you? You're only a voice on the telephone, and you claim to be Catherine Martin. For all I know you may be wanted in fifteen countries for obtaining money under false pretenses. See you at the Vittoria one time or another."

I gathered that she had a lot of things to say to that, but I wasn't waiting for them. I hung up and headed for the street. Mr. Smartass Martin came after me.

"The police," he said, "will ask questions, and they'll get the reward."

"It'll be a great day for them. They're grossly underpaid."

"You're biting off your nose to spite your face."

"I do it all the time. I have a double-jointed chin."

"If this is your way of bargaining, we're prepared to be generous."

Since this was ambulatory dialogue, it had at this point carried us all the way to where I had Baby parked. When I climbed into her, he did a double take, but I could see that it wasn't until I had come up with the ignition key and had her purring that he really came around to believing it. He changed his tone, and I didn't like the change. I don't go for anybody measuring his manners on a scale of the price bracket of the wheels I roll. You know, disdainful with Datsuns and polite with Porsches.

"Look," he said, "if you got the impression I was being rude, I apologize."

"If it's worrying you, put it in writing. Miss Martin can bring it along when she comes around to the Vittoria."

Pushing an apology was evidently not in his line. He climbed right back to his toplofty perch.

"How do we know that you are at this hotel nobody ever heard of or even that there is any such place?"

"You don't."

Since this seemed as good an exit line as any, I pulled Baby away from the curb and left him standing.

It's only a short walk from the Excelsior to the Vittoria. They are both on Partenope. They both have the same view of the bay and both offer the same comforts. They are, nevertheless, worlds apart, the full distance from the Martin world of glitter, fawning flunkies, and international homogenization to the Erridge world of everything a man can need unless he's afflicted with an indecent yen for battalions of bowers and scrapers.

The short walk, of course, is a somewhat longer ride, but that's only because of the one-way traffic setup, and we've already been through all that. I tooled around to the Vittoria. The desk clerk provided the necessary manila envelope, and I sealed up the passport and the lira in it. He deposited the envelope in the hotel safe. The coolie bag with the rest of her stuff I took up to my room. I washed my hands and, before they were dry, the phone rang.

It was the desk clerk. Miss Catherine Martin was in the lobby asking for me. He's a good man, that desk clerk, but he is a man and he is a Neapolitan. Just from the way he sounded, I could tell that he had taken stock of Miss Catherine Martin's physical assets and that the stock-taking had upped his respect for Matthew Erridge all the way to the level of something like awe and reverence.

I gave it the casual touch.

"You can send her up," I said.

It was only a couple of moments before the phone rang again. The lady wasn't coming up. She wanted me to come down. I had pretty well expected that, but there's nothing wrong with testing.

"Okay," I said. "If she doesn't mind waiting."

He shifted into Italian.

"Do I ask her?" he said.

"No. You tell her. She has her choice. She can come up or she can wait."

He didn't ask me if I had lost my mind, but from the way he sounded, I knew he was thinking it.

"It must be that you haven't seen her," he said.

"Nice to look at, isn't she?"

"Mamma mia!"

"Exactly. So with my compliments, enjoy it."

"Tanto grazie, Signor."

"Prego."

We're friends, that desk clerk and I, but we never forget our manners. It's always the thank you and you're welcome but not often with the degree of fervor he had put into this particular *grazie*.

I took a long look at myself in the bathroom mirror. The shave was all right, but I hadn't given any deep thought to my choice of tie that morning. It was an all-right tie but I was certain I could do better. I checked the ties in my closet and brought out some of the Atkinsons and a few of the Romagnolis to see how they might go with the jacket and the shirt and the weather and the occasion. At least three or four were so good that it was difficult to decide between them.

After considerable deliberation I settled on one. I took my time tying it. It was a great tie and on any occasion it would merit a great knot, and this wasn't just any occasion. I also had time to kill. I knew that in the *Taming of the*

Shrew Petruchio took time to make himself unkempt but, with all due respect to Shakespeare, I didn't feel I had to be that slavish in following the script.

Eventually, satisfied that I'd done my best, I looked at my watch. I had been the better part of ten minutes and I was riding a hunch that Catherine Martin had never before in her young life been kept waiting even five minutes. Also, it was reaching the place where I would have shown the desk clerk sufficient kindness. There does have to be a limit even to generosity.

I took the wrapping paper and string off a package of something I'd bought the day before and I made a neat parcel of the coolie bag. I'd had enough of parading hotel lobbies with the thing out in plain sight. I knew that handbags for men had been getting big in the fashion world, but I've never been that far into that world. I have yet to feel any crying need for a handbag.

I'm a pocket man myself. Remember how handy I was with the pipe, Charlie? Try and put that one over if you've been carrying all your stuff around in a purse.

I went down to the lobby. The peachcake was there. She was a stormy-looking peachcake and she was tapping her foot. She spotted me on sight and that was flattering. I hadn't known that she had been noticing me during that time in the bank when I had been noticing her.

"Oh," she said. "It's you."

"Catherine Martin?" I asked.

"Stop putting on an act. You know perfectly well I'm Catherine Martin."

"Do you have any identification? Naples is a lovely city but it does have a shocking crime rate. It's best to be absolutely sure."

"How can I have any identification when you have it?"

I gave it the sympathetic touch.

"That does put you in a difficult position. Tell me. Just what can I do for you?"

"You can stop clowning and give me back my bag."

"I tried to do that. It's too bad you weren't available."

"I just don't know what you want."

"Would it knock you over if I told you I don't want anything?"

"You must want something."

"You know the wrong kind of people, Catherine Martin. I hope you won't mind if I don't call you Cuddles. Any time I catch myself using a word like that, I have to wash my mouth out with soap."

She wanted nothing so much at that moment as to walk away from it, but she couldn't. I had her passport.

"I suppose you read the letter."

That had to be the best insult she could think up on the spur of the moment. Her tone let me know the contempt she felt for men who read other people's mail.

"You do know the wrong kind of people. Your passport gave me your name. The envelope gave me your Naples address. It made it easy to get your things back to you, or at least it should have made it easy. The envelope also warned me that you might be cutesy-poo. It didn't warn me that you might be difficult."

"My brother told you there'd be a reward. What more do you want?"

"No reward, but a lot more. Something real big, something that would tax you Martins terribly, something like common courtesy."

"I'd like to know how you got my bag."

"I saw you lose it. I thought you'd like to have it back. I chased the kids, caught up with them, and took it away from them. It's as simple as that."

For a moment she looked embarrassed, maybe even

ashamed, but it was only the moment. She rose above it. She smiled. It was the first time for me, seeing her smile.

You should have seen it, Charlie. It lit up the whole lobby. I promised myself that I was going to see a lot of this girl and I was going to work at thinking up ways to make her smile.

"A knight in shining Porsche," she said.

I pushed the parcel at her.

"Your coolie kit," I said.

She took it as though it was the least important thing going.

"I can't bring up anything about the reward again," she said. "I see now that was insulting, and I'm sorry. I'm humiliated. I've been a stinker and I'm ashamed of myself. You've been more than kind, and certainly it isn't enough just to say thank you. There must be something I can do."

"There is. You can open it up and check to see if it's all there."

"I wouldn't think of it. It would just be more insult."

"It would be simple common sense. You should want to know and I do want to know."

She smiled again.

"All right. If you want me to . . ."

She undid the string and folded back the paper. Lifting the bag out of the wrapping, she tucked it under her arm. With the strap broken she couldn't hang it from her shoulder.

"Check to see if everything's there."

"I'm sure it is. See? I trust you."

"This is your day for making mistakes. Right now you could be making another."

"You think I can't learn."

"I think you'll need a lot of teaching. So, go ahead now. Check."

She took the bag from under her arm and spread it open and all along making a big show of doing something stupid and unnecessary just to indulge Erridge. Then quickly her look changed. I had her confused, off base, uncertain. She didn't know what to think.

"You're a strange man," she said. "Those boys on the motorcycle could have taken the money and you didn't get it back from them, but they didn't keep the passport and the letter. You had those. Otherwise . . ."

"Otherwise I might have known your hotel by guessing you were the Excelsior type, but there was no way I could have known about Cuddles."

The chill went back on.

"I would like my passport, please. The letter doesn't matter and the money doesn't matter much, but the lost passport is a nuisance."

I went to the desk and spoke to the clerk. She was following me with her eyes. She was clearly confused and troubled. The troubled look wasn't nearly as good as the smile, but that doesn't mean it wasn't lovely to look at.

The clerk pulled the envelope out of the safe. I handed it to her.

"The money doesn't matter much to you," I told her, "but it will matter a lot to your insurance company. The more they have to pay out on losses, the higher the premiums go. I know that wouldn't matter to you, but it will be rough on other people who want to be insured. You ought to learn to think of them."

"You are a strange man. You play the most peculiar games. I can't understand what for."

She was doing it again, dropping the sealed envelope into her bag without so much as opening it, again taking it on faith that everything was going to be there.

"I'll tell you what for, but first you're going to check the envelope and make certain there's nothing still missing."

Now it was an air of bored, long-suffering patience, but she did do as she was told. She broke the seal on the envelope and looked inside it.

"Nothing missing," she said. "Passport, letter, and money. Now what?"

"You count the money."

"All those silly lira?"

"For millions of people who need them and don't have them they're not silly."

Unaccountably that brought the smile back.

"You know what you're like?" she said.

"You told me. A knight in shining Porsche."

"Yes. That, of course, but right now you're like somebody's father. Not mine, because Puddles was never stern or sensible or any of that, but like some other people's fathers, the you-children-don't-know-the-value-of-a-dollar kind."

"Your father wasn't that kind?"

"Puddles? Anything but."

"How could he be if you called him Puddles? My kind of father would have smacked that out of you the first time you said it."

"He liked it. It kept him feeling young."

"Even infantile," I said. "But what about me? Don't you think I might like to feel young? Telling me I'm like somebody's father. That was unkind. It's worse than a girl telling me she wants me to be a brother to her."

"You don't need anything to make you feel young, because you are young. If you like, though, I could call you Muddles. It will be confusing, of course, because it's what we used to call Mother; but she's gone. She won't mind."

"No use making things confusing. I would mind. I don't

want to be anyone's father, and I'm all wrong for being your mother. So just call me Matt. I'll like that."

"I like it, too," she said.

"Good. Then that's settled. You still have to count the money."

"Yes, Matt."

She was about to bring that great wad of lira out of the envelope and flash it around in public. Putting my hand over hers, I shoved the money back into the envelope. It came to me as a shock that it was the first time I had touched this girl. It had to be, because the charge I got from having her hand in mine was not the kind of thing a man could ever forget. I hadn't had anything like that before. I had to work at remembering what I'd been about to tell her. I would just as soon have kept things as they were, just staying there forever with her hand in mine. I made an effort.

"Not here," I said. "Not out in public. You wondered what games I was playing. This had been one of them, hoping to teach you that there are people who have nothing, and from where they sit, Catherine Martin has too much. You don't rub their noses in it."

"And what are your other games?" she asked.

"That's for later. First you will have counted the lira."

"But not here. Do I hide away in the ladies with it?" She giggled. "I don't know about hotels like this. Do they have paper? The ones in the gas stations sometimes don't."

I'd known of tourists who showed their contempt for devalued currency by lighting their cigars with it, but I'd thought that wobbly dollars might have knocked that nonsense off. Evidently this girl hadn't noticed what had been happening to the dollar. Hers had the strength of numbers.

"There is paper," I said. "You won't have to use your

lira, but you'll be more comfortable counting it up in my room."

That made her giggle some more.

"Your other games," she said.

I fished my room key out of my pocket and handed it to her.

"You go up alone," I said. "I'll wait down here."

She pushed the key back into my hand.

"No," she said. "I was well brought up. I don't go up to a man's room alone. I'll go up with you."

I looked at the key.

"Either you have a compulsion to live dangerously or you think that I'm that much like somebody's father."

She laughed. This time it wasn't just a giggle. It was a complete laugh.

"When I was at school," she said, "it was when I was about fifteen. My roommate's parents were in Nassau and I flew down with her for a weekend. Her father kept making passes at me. The night before we were going back to school he tried to rape me."

"What stopped him or wasn't he stopped?"

"He was so fat and funny, I couldn't stop laughing. So nothing happened, and he's hated me ever since."

"And with good reason," I said. "Okay. Come upstairs if that's what you want."

"You wanted me to count the lira," she said, "so I won't be able to claim afterward that you kept any of it. I want you to watch me count it so that if any of it is missing, you won't be able to say I tucked some of it inside my bra because I wanted to frame you."

"You aren't wearing a bra."

"You noticed?"

"When I'm working, I'm an engineer. By professional training I have a sharp eye for stuff like structural support."

Up in the room she wandered about, looking at things and touching things. I hadn't put the ties away before I went down to her. The one I'd taken off and the others I'd brought out to choose from were lying on the bed where I had dropped them.

With a smile that could have been a little less self-satisfied she sorted them out. It took her only a moment to zero in on the one I'd been wearing earlier that morning.

"This one wasn't bad," she said, "but the one you're wearing now is sexier."

Sexy regimental stripes, Charlie? Each of us to his own aphrodisiacs, I suppose.

"Count your lira," I told her.

She wasn't ready for that yet. She hadn't finished her researches into how the lower classes live. She inspected my bathroom. I guess she wanted to know whether there really was paper.

"I like your room, Matt," she said. "I like your hotel."

"If it was a flophouse, do you think I would have asked you up?"

"Of course, you would. You would because you would think that I would think I was too good for it and you would have to show me that I wasn't."

Maybe you think you know all there is to know about women, but any time you come down with that delusion, look out, brother. That's when they're going to surprise you. They get you to believing there's nothing under the hairdo but marshmallow fluff and then—whammo! They let you know there's a thinking machine and all the time it's been charging along in overdrive.

I told her to settle down and count her money. She took it to the writing table and counted it.

"It's all here, or anyhow I think it is."

"Don't you know?"

"I didn't count it before, but I'm sure it's all right."

"The bank gives you an exchange slip. It tells you what you're getting."

"Oh, those. I never look at them."

I told her where the exchange stood that morning.

"At school did they teach you arithmetic?" I asked.

"Multiplication. I'm a whiz at multiplication."

"All you need. Let's see you do some whizzing. Multiply the exchange rate by the dollars."

I offered her my pen. She pushed the pen back at me.

"Let me show off a little. I can do it in my head. I tack on two zeros and multiply by five."

"Or you can tack on three zeros and divide by two."

She thought about that for a moment.

"That's cute," she said. "It's easier that way."

She took a creditably short time for doing the calculation. Then she grinned at me.

"It's all here," she said.

"Good," I told her. "Now you stow it away and you say a nice thank you."

"Thank you isn't enough. You've been kind and you've been to a lot of trouble and you've been patient. I must do something nice for you."

"Like letting me take you to lunch," I suggested.

"Thank you, yes, but don't you want to kiss me?"

"Yes, but even more I want to spank you."

She took my hand and, turning it palm up, she inspected it. Then she slid her hand up my arm and took a feel of the muscle. Shaking her head, she stepped away from me.

"We better go to lunch," she said.

I know what you're thinking. What makes with old Erridge? Has he lost his mind or is it his balls? I was half thinking it myself as we went downstairs and out of the hotel, but the other half of my thinking told me that it had to wait till I could be sure it wasn't going to make her laugh. When I turned my key in at the desk the clerk murmured a few congratulatory words, and all I could do was promise myself that the time was going to come when I would have earned them.

Outside the hotel, settled in the Porsche, I did kiss her before I pulled Baby away from the curb. It was good, Charlie. It rang bells. It sent up Roman candles. The best of it was I could feel she was with me. She was also hearing the bells and seeing the fireworks.

While we were tooling along Partenope, she was silent for a while. I let myself believe she was thinking about me and about the kiss, and maybe she was for part of the time. When she spoke, though, it was all practical.

"I'm going to need a new bag," she said. "Are you one of those men who hates shopping, Matt?"

"I'm one of those men who likes being with you, anywhere, any time, doing anything."

"But you don't like shopping."

"I can think of things I like better."

She knew the shop she wanted and when I pulled up there, she took command.

"You wait in the car," she said. "I won't be long."

"Not long," I asked, "before you're out a back door and away?"

"Without my lunch? Don't be silly. I adore food. It's just that if you go in with me, I'll take forever making a decision. You're too distracting."

It wasn't a long wait and it may have seemed even shorter than it was because while I was waiting I had something to watch and something to think about.

It was the other Martin, at the wheel of a Rolls parked behind me, at a discreet distance with a couple of other cars parked between us. Aboard those wheels he looked natural enough. You know, to the manner born and to the bread bred, but he had company with him. They were taking their ease in the Rolls, but they didn't look at all natural there. I couldn't think of any vehicle in which they would look natural, nothing this side of a paddy wagon. They looked native and they looked to be every menacing inch what those two kids on the motorcycle undoubtedly aspired to be, tough, vicious, and dangerous. Keeping company like that, he could easily be separated from his car. Almost as easily he could be separated from his head. All it might take, after all, would be an overenthusiastic throat slitting.

They stayed there all the time I was waiting for Cathy. Since I haven't the kind of stomach that could take Cuddles, I'd begun to call her Cathy in my head. If cows chew cuds, would calves chew cuddles? I was going to have to ask her that sometime.

When she came out, she had shed the maimed coolie job and had replaced it with a Gucci. Nobody could say the kid didn't have range.

I hopped out and opened the door for her. She flung her arms around me and kissed me with ostentatious enthusiasm before she got in. I settled her in the car and I settled myself beside her and then there was a kiss that I initiated. Just as we came up out of it, the Rolls came cruising past us. Brother gave us the thumbs-up signal as he went sailing by, but if I hadn't been looking for them, I would never have known that his two buddies were still in the car. They were crouched down all but out of sight. Only the tops of their two curly heads were sticking up in view.

"Oh, look," Cathy said. "There goes Huddles. He's been following us. I guess he's convinced now that you're all right."

"You've been seeing him?" I asked. "He isn't alone."

"Oh, them." Her dismissal couldn't have been airier. "Hired muscle. Now that he knows he doesn't need them, he'll just pay them off and send them on their way. Huddles does that all the time. At the drop of a hat. I keep telling him that it's silly or it's TV poisoning or something like that, but he seems to get a charge out of doing it. You know what I think? I think it makes him feel real."

"The types he's got there," I told her, "could make him feel dead."

"They weren't for him," she said. "They were for you, but that was before I had any idea that you would be you, if you know what I mean."

I had an approximation of an idea. I let it lay.

"Huddles," I said. "Henry, Herbert, Harold, Hezekiah?"

"Hugh."

"Mom is Muddles. Pop is Puddles. Cathy is Cuddles. Hugh is Huddles. There had to be a brother, Philip, or a sister, Phoebe, or did you do without Fuddles?"

"There never was more than the two of us except, of course for Puddles and Muddles. We came together, Huddles and I. We were a one-stork job, twins, and after that Muddles said she could never go through that again, and she never had to because I don't think Puddles had the energy. I've never known how he managed it even the one time and two of us at that, but we were enough for him."

I took her to Da Ciro for lunch. She'd never been there. It figured. It was too much the real Italian thing to have been on the Martin beat. She liked it and it wasn't just that she said so. She tucked into everything, but when it came to the fragolini, she was little-girl greedy. Watching her eat those wild strawberries, you could have thought that she hadn't gone all her life without ever knowing what it is to be hungry.

III.

We had fun in Naples. She'd been to Pompeii. I took
her to Herculaneum. She'd been to Capri. I took her to
Ischia. We swam. We sailed. We night-lifed. Now and then,
here and there, we ran into Huddles. For some reason that
I've never stopped to explore, calling him that didn't bother
me. It just didn't seem to have the nausea potential exerted
by Cuddles.

There could have been some awkwardness, but there
wasn't. He never referred to our first meeting. He gave it
the we've-always-been-friends touch, and I was happy
enough to leave it that way. I've never had any Hatfield or
McCoy in me. Protracted feuding wasn't the Erridge style,
and I discovered early that if I was going to be seeing
Cathy, Huddles would be unavoidable. They were, after all,
as she liked to put it, wombmates. They had begun life as
close as a pair of siblings can be (unless you want to hit me
with oddities like Siamese twins), and they had remained
close ever since.

Maybe the closeness persisted because they had it so
nicely adjusted. He went his way and she went hers. So you
can read that for we went ours. It was all right, but somehow I could never get away from the feeling that he was always there. She was enjoying herself with me, but Huddles

was home base. We were temporary. They were permanent.

If he was alone when we met up, he would stop and speak. Sometimes he had a drink with us or even a meal. A couple of times it grew to more than that. We'd make it a threesome, swimming or sailing. It never seemed to be by prearrangement. We'd run into him one place or another and it would just happen, though once or twice I did wonder if it could be as accidental as they made it seem. It hardly mattered since it wasn't all of the time or even any great part of it.

There were the times when he would stop by with us for only a few minutes, on his way to something else. There were also the times when he would just wave as he went by or smile and nod from across a room and then pull away before there could be anything more.

Those were the times when he wasn't alone. I never saw him with anybody I didn't recognize on sight. It wasn't that his companions were ever people that I knew. It was always maybe what you could call a species recognition.

Huddles, I could see, liked to play out of his league. Whether his company was female or male, it was always tough, always hard babies from the other side of the tracks, but, more than that, always of a type I'd be careful not to turn my back on.

The way I saw it, if any of the men weren't pimps, it would have to be because, with good reason, Huddles had mistaken them for it. If any of the babes weren't prostitutes, it would have to be because, regardless of what he had in his pants, they knew that what he had in his pockets was a lot of what they wanted. They were ready to earn it even as beginners.

Since I was trying to work away from the somebody's-father image, I said nothing about it to Cathy. Also, it might have been that I had an uncomfortable touch of some feeling that the wombmates might be seeing me as her equivalent of the company he kept. She let him have his fun. He was letting her have hers.

It came up, therefore, only when she brought it up. She wanted to dance. We went to a place she picked and Huddles was there. He spotted us as we came in and he gave us the smile and the nod. This time he was part of a foursome. The two dames were a long way from being Sophia Loren, but they could have been the originals of some of the grubbier characters she's played. The other guy was noisily and unmistakably an American. He was wearing a jacket that had the whole place lit up. It was a print job of remotely Paisley inspiration, but if the pattern did come out of India, it could only have come by way of the wallpaper in one of those Montmartre hotel rooms that are up for twenty-minute rentals.

His taste in clothes, furthermore, was the least of what was wrong with him. He had his arm around one of the girls and, since she was a hefty hunk of womanflesh, he had to reach just a little too far to get around her. He had short, thick arms—a lot of power there but not much reach. Just by eye I would have said he'd measure for something like a seventeen collar shirt size, and with a thirty-two sleeve length he'd have to wear sleeve garters to keep his cuffs up off his knuckles.

Stretching strained his shirt buttons and pulled his Paisley job wide open, more than wide enough to show a shoulder holster and the blued steel of a revolver butt.

I've seen off-duty fuzz back home in the States when they'd made the accidental show of their weaponry. That's police regulations in our gun-happy republic: A cop must have his service revolver on him even when he's off duty. Loudmouth could have been a cop and he couldn't have been more off duty, but those police regulations don't reach out of the home territory. He was an ocean and more away from any police regulations that might have applied to him. He had to be wearing the thing for reasons of his own.

After giving us the standard nod and smile, Huddles went into his standard routine. He leaned across his babe and whispered a couple of hurried words to his fellow American. Then, while he was getting *il conto* and paying it, his buddy was dragging the girls to their feet and starting to herd them to the door. Since at that very same time we were being taken to a table, we passed the little convoy on the way. The passing was so close that it only just missed being body contact.

The women were taking no notice of us, but our fellow countryman gave us the head-to-foot runover. His interest in Cathy seemed to be limited; he concentrated on me. Ever been in a bar where you've seen a guy who's hungry for a fight? He has nothing against anyone in particular. He's not finding anyone who is about to help him along by giving offense. He's going to have to toss a fist into anything that comes his way and he's looking over the available candidates. That was the way this character looked at me.

We were installed at our table by the time Huddles had dispensed the lira. So when he headed straight for the door, he wasn't passing anywhere near us.

Cathy chuckled.

"Huddles," she said. "He's so funny and old-fashioned."

"Old-fashioned?"

"Didn't you see him with those people just now?"

"I saw him."

"It's the same every time he's with anybody."

"What's the same?"

As if I didn't know.

"He won't come near me, not if he's with anybody. He shields pure, innocent, little me from any contact with the wicked world. The wicked world is out there for men to play in, but little girls have to be protected from it. Huddles of all people, so Victorian."

"You want to play out there?" I asked.

"No. I'm happy where I am."

I couldn't have asked for a better answer, and that answer was a large part of the reason I went to Sicily. I have nothing against Sicily. Any time you are looking for a European play pen, you can do a lot worse than Sicily. And when a girl like Cathy tells you she likes being with you and if you are to go on being with her, it will have to be in Sicily, there are compulsions, Charlie, urgent compulsions.

The idea of taking off for Palermo wasn't hers. It came from Huddles and it came all of a sudden. She wasn't crazy for it. She wanted to stay on in Naples. I like to think that was because Erridge was there, but then all too readily she suggested that, if they were going to go anywhere, it ought to be Sardinia. Everybody was there.

Sardinia was all too much the place that year. The Aga Khan had bought a large hunk of it and had dressed it up to meet every possible jet-set need. I hadn't taken any particular notice of the envelope of the letter she'd had tucked in her passport, but it seemed to me that it had worn a Sardinia postmark. What followed between her and Huddles made it seem even more likely that it was as I thought. I began thinking of everybody as Everybody.

"We came to Naples because you wanted to get away from everybody," Huddles reminded her.

"But that was before."

"What's going to make it different now?"

"Matt will."

"When did I say I was going to Sardinia?" I asked.

She let me have the smile, turning it on me both barrels.

"You haven't yet," she said.

Huddles sighed.

"And what Cuddles wants Cuddles gets."

I didn't know who Everybody was, but whoever he was, Cathy had plans for him. She was going to play games and in the playing, she was figuring on leading with one Matthew Erridge.

I had a whole parcel of reasons that were telling me I didn't want to go to Sardinia. It would be Cuddles and Huddles heavily multiplied. Running around with me, she had been sloughing off a lot of Little Miss Richbitch stuff. I could just see her in Sardinia back up to her ears in it. That was going to be a big pain.

This last bit made me dig in and say no Sardinia. Erridge doesn't go for being used. That was one of the things she was going to have to learn. She could count on me not being manipulative, but she was overdue for learning that she could also count on me refusing to be manipulated.

"Not this time," I said. "Everybody's Sardinia is not my Sardinia. No way."

She didn't even pull a pout. Her heart hadn't been set on it. It was Huddles who reacted. He grinned all over his face.

"Then what about Sicily?" he asked.

"I know worse places."

"If it's Sicily, you'll come with us?" Cathy asked.

"Why go anywhere?"

"Why stay here?" Huddles countered.

It was a better question than he could know. I had already stayed on in Naples longer than I had planned. I suppose that's a bad way to put it. I'd been drifting, and as soon as you have plans it isn't drifting any more. On the other hand, once you settle down, it isn't drifting either. If it hadn't been for Cathy, I would have moved on by this time. Where I don't know, but somewhere. So why not Sicily?

We went around and around about it and things began to come clear. Huddles was going to Sicily and nobody was going to stop him. He had something going for him there, or he thought he had. This wasn't just a whim that could easily be replaced by another whim. He was going to go. Another thing, Cathy would go with him. She might grumble, but she would go. They kept each other on a long leash, but there was no complete letting go.

It it came down to a Naples-with-Erridge or-Sicily-with-Huddles choice, Erridge would fade out. Cathy would revert to being Cuddles and she'd go to Sicily. Maybe it was no fault of mine, but I had a feeling that if I hadn't said that uncompromising no to Sardinia, she would have put up a better fight. Huddles might have come around, and what Cuddles wanted Cuddles would get.

If I was right about that, then I had to recognize that I'd had at least some part in the decision's going to Huddles. So some of it was that I liked what I had going with her, and some of it was that I began to feel responsible. On what I could make of his sudden itch to move, it had to be that among those bimbos quaint, old, Victorian Huddles was careful not to introduce to his sister someone had held out a promise in Sicily of something Huddles thought was going to be great stuff. Experience, knowledge of the world, gut instinct—everything was telling me that Huddles was heading for trouble. I couldn't read it that he was running out on trouble. If it had been that, he would have been happy enough to go anywhere. One place would have been as good as another as long as it was away.

Since it had to be Sicily and no place else, it seemed clear that he was running to and not from.

So far as I was concerned, his trouble could be all his. I had no intention of setting up to be my girl's brother's keeper, but Cathy would be going with him, and how could it be that his trouble wouldn't be her trouble? And that, I was expecting, would be the least of it.

For all his precautions—and I had to grant that he had thus far been taking them—it could be just too easy for him to get her involved. If somebody should want to exercise maximum leverage on him, where would they go if not to Cathy?

So there it was. Whatever it was going to be, I had to go along and keep an eye on her. I had to try and do what I could for her. I suppose I didn't want to think that I could be a man who would be no more good to her than that Everybody up in Sardinia.

We went to Sicily. We were on the Naples-Palermo car-ferry that very same night. When the Martins take a notion to move, they move fast.

There was never a suggestion that we wouldn't take both cars. Two cars were necessary if they were to follow their practice of each going his own way. Since it was being assumed that her way would be mine, I wasn't knocking it. It was obvious that it couldn't be often, and never for long, that she wouldn't have some man around who provided her with wheels. If it wasn't Erridge or that Everybody up in Sardinia, it would inevitably be some other guy somewhere.

She did tell me, though, that back home there always were more than enough cars to go around, and in travel when they were down to just the one paltry Rolls, it was hers any time she needed it. Huddles would hire a car for his own use during such between-men interludes. That was one thing about Cathy. She had that honesty. She never let me think that I'd been the first, and she made it equally clear that I wouldn't be the last. Forever was too long. It would get to be a bore. She didn't need permanence. There was always Huddles, and she never had the first doubt that there always would be Huddles.

Palermo is a good town, but nobody wanted to hang around there. It's a city and Naples had given us enough of cities for a while. That Cathy wanted to move along to some place where we could swim seemed reasonable enough, but Huddles had me wondering. The first suggestion that we move straight on to the south coast came not from her but from him. That this lad should have had too much of cities seemed incomprehensible. I couldn't believe that his insistence on Sicily had been in pursuit of nothing more than country pleasures. He was in no way that breed of cat. I couldn't believe that I'd been wrong about him, but he had me baffled.

It was his idea that we hit the *autostrada* that cuts straight across the island from north coast to south coast— Palermo to Catania. From there it's only a short run along the coast to Taormina. That *autostrada* is great for getting from here to there, but it's nowhere. Superhighways anywhere are superhighways and nothing more.

I was for going the longer way around—Monreale, Segesta, Selinunte, Agrigento, Siracusa, Taormina. Doing it that way, you start with the Normans and then hit the great string of places where the old Greeks were. Conquerors or colonists, those old babies who pulled up stakes and went to Sicily were the wild boys of their time, the itchy-footed, lusty lads who gladly left the quiet of home to strike out for the places that were far and new. What they left behind them, even if it's only ruins, has the mark of their wildness on it and the strength of their gutsiness.

I wanted Cathy to see all that. What's more, I wanted to be the one who showed it to her. I'd taken her to Hercula-

neum, and the way she'd gone for that had told me she was
my kind of girl. My kind of a girl deserved more than the
quick run down a superhighway.

"It'll take a month to get anywhere," Huddles complained.

"More like a week."

"All right, a week. It'll seem like a month."

"I don't care about getting anywhere," Cathy told him.
"I want to be places."

Spoken like my girl.

"We'll get to Taormina and you'll be there."

"You take the *autostrada,* and we'll join up with you
down there in a week or two," I suggested.

He looked to Cathy. It had to be all right with her.

"No," she said.

"Why not? You'll be all right with Matt."

"I know I'll be all right. What about you?"

This was new. She hadn't given any hint of this before.
Suddenly she was shortening the leash. This could be why
she gave up on Sardinia so easily. Her beloved Huddles had
to be watched over and protected. It startled him as much
as it did me.

He paused a moment while he was giving her one of
those looks that tries to see inside a person and that always
fails. After a moment he gave up on it.

"I'm a big boy," he said.

"You're a big dope. I don't know who's in Taormina, but
call her up and tell her to wait or tell her to come up here.
You'll have room for her in the Rolls."

"Very funny."

But that was it. What Cuddles wants, Cuddles gets.

When we started off, he was sulking. Since, however, he
was doing it in his car and she was riding with me in the
Porsche, he wasn't impressing anybody with it.

At Monreale he did tag around with us and he worked hard at being bored by the mosaics. I've never known anyone else who saw them who wasn't knocked out, but Huddles put a lot of sweat into his boredom. At Segesta he left us to ourselves. It's a high place, wild and windy, where the temple ruins stand, and then it's a climb to an even higher place where the theater looks down on miles and miles of valley.

Cathy climbed up there with me.

"A theater is a theater is a theater," Huddles muttered and stayed down below.

We hung on up there a while. Coming down, I was watching the path, holding on to Cathy and steering her around the spots where the footing wasn't the safest. So she saw it before I did.

I had her by the arm, and I felt her hesitate and stiffen. I looked at her but she had gone away from me. She was looking down below where there was a little stand for selling postcards and stuff.

Huddles was there but not on the path in front of it where it would have been natural for any visitor to be. He was behind it where there was nothing. Let's change that a little to say there was nothing but concealment. If we hadn't been looking down on him from above he would have been well hidden.

He was not alone. There was another man with him. For recognizing people our angle wasn't good. We were looking all but straight down on them. I couldn't see much more than thick, black, curly hair and a broad span of heavy shoulders, but nevertheless, I thought I had a make on the character. If it wasn't one of the pair he'd had with him in the Rolls that first day, then it had to be some other so much of the same breed that it would make little difference.

I promised myself a better look when we got down to a

lower level, but the path took a turn that for several yards put the stand and the area behind it out of our view. Then another turn brought it back in and they weren't there any more. The two of them had vanished or at least had moved to some place that was out of our line of sight.

When we finished the descent to the temple level, Huddles was waiting for us at the foot of the path. The other man was nowhere to be seen. Huddles, however, was a changed man. He was in a conspicuously happier mood.

"Good theater?" he asked.

"Great."

I'd left it to Cathy to answer him.

"What were they playing up there? *Uncle Tom's Cabin? Abie's Irish Rose? East Lynn?*"

"The show was down here. Who was your sneaky friend?"

He didn't let the question bother him. She was forgetting their way of doing things. Mildly he reminded her.

"Questions, Cuddles?" he said.

She shrugged.

"All right. No questions, but then I'm right. It is like that."

"But it isn't. I'm just asserting a principle."

"Okay, okay. Objection noted and sustained. Satisfied?"

"Since there's no reason why you shouldn't know, he was just a man who needed a light."

"For a joint, of course, or wasn't that why you couldn't give him his light without going into hiding?"

"More questions, Cuddles?"

"You could tell me to mind my own business. I hate it when you lie to me. I never lie to you."

"I don't ask questions."

"All right. Sorry. I didn't ask. Skip it."

"But you did ask and again, except for the principle of the thing, I don't mind answering."

"I don't want to hear."

She put her hands to her ears. It's a good gesture, but it doesn't do much in the way of blocking out sound.

"The wind blows like crazy up here. We had to find some shelter before he could get the light."

She said nothing. She was pretending that she had deafened herself completely with her hands. If she was aware that the back of that stand was the windier side, she gave no sign of it.

Whatever that meeting had been, however, it provided unexpected dividends. For the greater part of our long way around to Taormina we had the company of a transformed Huddles. He had come out of his sulks. He was good, cheerful company. It could have been that it was bugging him that he had lied to Cathy and he was trying to make amends.

That might have been enough to bring about the change in him, but I couldn't wipe out the thought that there was more to it than that. It wasn't only that he had switched to trying to go along with Cathy and me on everything. The tension and the anxiety had gone out of him, and it hadn't been a gradual thing. It was the sudden miracle.

I couldn't explain it unless it might be that he'd had a message, reassurance that whatever he was looking to find in Taormina would still be waiting for him. Earlier on he had been too worried and restless to allow himself to enjoy anything. Now that he was relaxed, he did begin to enjoy himself.

At Selinunte, where the temples stand at the edge of the sea, he did the full round of the ruins with us and he wasn't merely trying. He was interested. Although I can't say his interest was undivided. He did keep looking back over his shoulder as though he might be expecting that he would be followed, but I couldn't see anything frightened or even apprehensive in his backward glances. He was just checking. So far as I could see, nobody showed, and again so far as I could see, it was making no great difference to him that nobody was showing.

Since I knew the road and he didn't, all the way from Palermo I'd had Baby in the lead and had been careful to pace myself so that Huddles in the Rolls wouldn't fall too far back and get lost at some unmarked road fork. The road along the south coast from Selinunte into Agrigento, however, is foolproof. Nothing intersects it or forks off from it except minor country tracks and it's well marked all the way.

When I say that soon after we pulled out of Selinunte he began falling back and within a couple of miles we could no longer see him behind us, you must understand that I wasn't gunning Baby along. I was in no hurry. I was holding her down to loafing speed, a pace at which he could have easily passed us and lost us in his wake.

If I was taking it easy, however, he was taking it easier. It seemed evident that he wanted to be alone, and since it didn't seem to be disturbing Cathy, it wasn't bugging me. This was nothing new. We were just back to our Naples style. He was going his way and we were going ours. Since we were going it along the same road, it could be done only through a difference in pace. It's a short run on a good road, not quite touching eighty miles, and since I took all of two and a half hours to do it, it hardly seemed possible that he could have taken all of an hour longer. For my money a Rolls is a rather staid and pompous set of wheels, but it is moved along by a good engine. It isn't drawn by oxen or water buffalo.

I was asking no questions, and either Cathy hadn't no-

ticed or she had already asked her questions for the day. He
turned up in good shape, blithe and happy and still his new
Selinunte self.

We stayed in Agrigento a couple of days, and while we
were there Huddles divided himself between his Naples
style and his new style. All day he tagged around with us
and gave every evidence of enjoying it. Come nightfall, he
would take off on his own and from his bleary-eyed but
well-satisfied morning look you had to conclude that overnight he had been doing all right for himself.

To come into a strange town and a provincial one at
that, one that could never have the lavish sin possibilities
available in a city like Naples, and immediately to get the
thing made called for either a great stroke of luck or prearranged contacts.

It could have been luck, but I just wasn't about to believe
it. Of course, he hadn't wanted to come this way through
Agrigento, and it seemed most unlikely that he would have
worked so hard at opposing the route if he had known he
was to have something going for him there.

I was remembering Segesta, his moving into the wind to
give that stranger a light and his change of mood after it.
Whatever he now had going for him in Agrigento had unquestionably been set up in those few moments behind the
souvenir shack. I was guessing that this guy who had
needed a light was operating as something like a circuit-rid-
ing pimp. If I was right about this being one of the men I
had seen with Huddles in Naples, then it was a reasonably
good bet that, since he was going to be a bit late in getting
to Taormina, he was now being provided with some stop-
gap enjoyments along the road.

So what? Boys will be boys. Live and let live. Love and
let love. Don't ask me why a line from an old Latin poet

kept coming at me. "Death tweaks my ear and tells me to live because he is coming."

That's a loused up translation, but I'm no poet, Charlie, and it should be near enough to give you the idea.

It could have been that what brought it to mind was our coming on the bodies, the one so newly dead and the other so irrevocably dying, but it seems to me that the line had been haunting me even before we had run on to that.

IV.

Just outside Agrigento on a back road east of the town there's a restaurant. It's no gourmet spot, not by a long shot, but Agrigento is no gourmet's mecca. For the area, this restaurant is as good as the best, which means you won't remember that they put anything in front of you that was inedible, and you won't remember that they served you anything that gave you any great pleasure. You'll eat adequately, and you'll promptly forget what it was you ate.

Nobody goes there for either the cuisine or the cellar. It's the place to go in the evening only because of its location. It sits on a stretch of flat country and fronts on this rutted, dusty road. All the place has is a view, and you have to look off into the distance for that. The immediate foreground is dull, flat, and unprofitable. Those aren't my words. They more or less belong to a better man, but they do describe the scene.

Off in the distance, though, the great line of Doric temples stands against the sky, and in the evening while you are at dinner, the ruins are illuminated. At that distance and flooded with carefully modulated light they show nothing of their wreckage, none of the scars of time and decay. They look almost as they must have looked twenty-five hundred years ago when the old gods were still living in them.

Since they are the main event and nothing is allowed to compete with them, all other illumination down that way is nothing or next to nothing. The restaurant keeps its lights low. The road that leads into it is totally black.

Cathy and I ate there both nights we stayed in Agrigento. Huddles wasn't with us either time. It was no kind of a night-life place. It had nothing going for it but the illuminated temples, but for most people that was enough. Huddles may not have been the only guy who ever came to Agriento for something else, but if there have been others, they would always have been a minority.

The first night we went, there were people and the food and the wine and the ruins, but like the food and the wine, the people were nothing for which you'd take your eyes off the temples even momentarily.

The second night was not too different, but that time there was something that caught my attention. It was the kind of thing that couldn't miss. In a way, I suppose, it was another version of Cathy that first day in the bank. It was a less well-bred version, but it was essentially the same thing.

It was a couple, middle-aged, overweight, and over dressed. There may have been a reason for the enormous expanse of her spread. The bigger the bosom, the more room for pinning on the diamonds. His then might have been taken on only through eating and drinking with her mouthful for mouthful.

Cathy and I had settled in there shortly after sunset and we were sucking on Camparis waiting for dusk to deepen to dark and the temple lights to come up. So when this pair arrived, we took them in. For the moment they were the only show in town. They had to have the best table, the one with the best view, and he was prepared to pay for it. The way the place was set up all the tables had an equally good view, but equal would never satisfy them. If anyone else had as good a seat for the show, it would spoil their enjoyment of it.

Since he had to have the best and since he was prepared to make it worth the waiter's while, the waiter pointed at one of the tables at random and elected that one the best. He settled them at it and the lovely lira passed from hand to hand. Then came the ordering. Item by item they discussed the menu, holding the waiter in unbroken attendance so he could answer their questions. Actually, it was always the same question repeated over and over.

"Is it fresh?"

Did they expect the waiter to tell them that everything was warmed over from the week before. I don't know, but it's a good bet that the answers didn't matter. The question was designed to let the whole world know that they would settle for nothing but the best that money could buy and that they had the money to buy it. Her diamonds, of course, were shouting it all over the place, but they couldn't do the rounds of the dining room to give every last one of us an eye check. How could they know that a blind man hadn't sneaked into the place?

After the waiter had sworn on his father's grave and his mother's virtue that every last thing was of the freshest, they made their choices and briefly let him go. As he came by Cathy and me, he winked and hissed the expected word.

"*Milanese.*"

It's the great Italian myth and it flourishes everywhere south of Milan. Anyone who is ostentatiously loaded and who throws his weight around even a little bit is immediately tagged for being a Milanese. He might be from Genoa or from Turin, but everybody would know that his soul lived in Milan.

Cathy was taking it all in.

"That first day in Naples," she said, "first in the bank and later in your hotel lobby you thought I was like that with my money."

"In a quieter, well-bred way. Yes."

She kicked me in the shin.

"You were supposed to say no."

"You can't stand it if Huddles lies to you, but you want me to. What makes me so different?"

"He's he and you're you."

"And that explains everything?"

"For me it does."

"To me it says Erridge doesn't count."

"I am fond of you. You do count, but not the way he does. It's no good your ever expecting that."

"If I was a guy who liked to wear his bitterness on his sleeve, I could say something about incest."

"You know that isn't true."

"I know. It's wombmates and that's never been baby talk for roommates, and way back there you were too young for it."

"Are you going to hold me accountable for the way I might have behaved when I was a fetus?"

"I don't want to hold you accountable for anything. I just want to hold you."

Between the talk taking that kind of a turn and the lights coming up on the temples, we pretty much wiped out the Milanese pair even though they never gave up on putting out their best efforts to make themselves the center of attention.

Maybe it was because they recognized that in competition with the illuminated temples they were losing out, or maybe it was just that even though they ate and drank far too much they also ate and drank much too fast, they were finished and out of there before any of the others of us that night. Cathy and I loitered over our dinner until it got to be lights-out time in temple zone. All the other patrons had come in after us and had been served after us. They were all still eating when Cathy and I pulled out.

We didn't go far, only to about fifty yards short of the place where that rutted back road would hook on to the highway. There we came on it, the wreckage of what had been one great hunk of fancy, custom-made automobile. It had gone off the road and rammed into a tree with maximum damage to tree, automobile, and occupants.

It was the pair of Milanese rich folks who had been in the restaurant. He must have been taking that rutted track at a speed for which it never had been built. Any Italian will tell you that's another Milanese trick, driving with a show-off dash without being possessed of any part of the necessary driving skills or even the quick enough reflexes. He was dead and, though she was still breathing, it seemed to me that she wasn't alive by much.

I sent Cathy back to the restaurant to tell them to phone for an ambulance.

"He's gone," I said, "and from the way she looks, she's going, but just in case there may be a chance."

I got Baby turned around for her because on that road it took a little too much doing. For the rest of it, since I'd let her drive a couple of times, I knew that she would be up to what it took. She was shaken, of course, but there was steel in that girl. I knew she'd be all right.

"I'll stay with them," she offered. "You go. You speak the language."

It was the last thing in the world she could have wanted but she felt she had to make the offer. It was something she was demanding of herself.

I turned her down.

"The waiter speaks English. Tell him. He'll make the call."

She took off and I couldn't have had it any other way. I had told her that the woman still had a little life in her, but I was saying nothing about the other thing I'd noticed. I hadn't been looking for it. In a situation like that it would need to have been the last thing to enter my mind, but it was too conspicuous. I couldn't help noticing.

The diamonds were gone. She had been stripped of them and not a single stone had been missed. The bracelets had been taken from her arms. The rings had been taken from her fingers. The pins had been ripped away from her dress. On this last, of course, I was just guessing. What with blood and the slicing action of shattered windshield glass, both the woman and her dress had been thoroughly hashed up, but unpinned or torn away, all the pins were gone.

Robbing the dead is nobody's pretty crime, but robbing a dying woman and leaving her to die, there's the double crime. Robbing her of her sparkling rocks would be the least of it. It was also robbing her of her remaining chance at life. Technically it might not be murder, but how could a man come closer?

The whole thing would need to have been quick. It hadn't been all that many minutes between their leaving the restaurant and the time Cathy and I pulled out. More than enough time for him to have cracked up his car, of course, and enough time for someone who happened to be right on hand to have gone all over the dying woman harvesting her diamonds.

All the odds had it that he wouldn't be hanging around, not with all that loot on him and the moment-to-moment expectation that other people would be coming down the road from the restaurant and that other people would quickly bring an ambulance and a major onslaught of fuzz.

On the other hand, I wasn't so sold on the odds of it that I would have considered letting Cathy stay there alone with the dead man and the dying woman while I went to call for the ambulance. He'd have to be crazily reckless to have gone on hanging around even for a minute after he'd finished gathering in her diamonds, but I couldn't make it for any other way than that he had been hanging around before the smashup.

I knew that it wasn't impossible for him to have been coming down to the highway and to have hit this turnoff just in time to be there for the crash. In that case he would have turned in on the dirt road to investigate the wreck. That certainly should have been the most reasonably believable guess on what had happened. Any other time and any other place it would have been the guess I'd have been making, but it was this time and this place and ever since Segesta I'd been carrying around a feeling that we were not alone.

Apart from the man we'd seen with Huddles behind the souvenir shack, I had seen no one. The hairs on the back of my neck, however, had all along felt as though they were standing up and pointing at someone. That's one of the things I've learned to trust, those hairs on the back of my neck. When they stand up and prickle, they are trying to talk to me. I try to listen.

Suppose the diamond haul had been serendipitous. Suppose someone was following us around this island. Suppose he had followed us to the restaurant and had established himself down here, where the side road joined the highway, waiting to pick us up again when we would be coming away from dinner. Then the smashup would have been opportunity for an unanticipated profit, and this would be a man who passed up no profit, anticipated or unanticipated.

If I was going to figure it that way, I had to figure that

Cathy and I—or maybe it was Cathy or I—had to be the main event. He scoops in the diamonds, but he's got to go on hanging around afterward because we could finish our dinner and go on our way and he would have lost us.

I very much wanted to look at the car and the tree and the road. I was wondering whether the accident might not have been as accidental as it looked, if in some way he hadn't caused the accident and perhaps I might be able to see some evidence of it, but there was the woman. Her breathing was shallow and irregular and her pulse was hard to find.

She was on the way out. You didn't have to be an M.D. to recognize that. There wasn't the first damn thing I could do for her. I was going to be much surprised if there would be anything anyone could do for her even if a guy with the medical know-how did get to her before these last few dregs of living had oozed away.

Still I was standing there with my hand on hers. Feeling for a pulse had landed it there and I just couldn't bring myself to take my hand away. It wasn't that I was giving myself any snow job like with my great, strong, magic hand I was holding her back from death. I knew better than that.

There have been wars and I have been in them. I've seen too much dying in my time and too much of it has been sudden. I have no delusions about it and I have no delusions about Erridge's powers.

Those hairs at the back of my neck were up and pointing, but this was a time when I couldn't be absolutely sure about them. We were out there in the dark, me and my hairs, alone with the dead and the dying. They could have been reacting to no more than that, those hairs of mine.

They got me to thinking about yet another possibility. If I should be right in this feeling I had that we were being followed and watched, would it be just one man on the two of us? How would he handle it if we were to separate? Of course, if he was tailing only one of us, either Cathy or me, he could be all right. He would just stay with the one he was watching.

Why was I thinking it was both of us being watched? That's easy. It was what I wanted to think. Two guys keeping an eye on the two of us, that could be nothing more than making sure we wouldn't happen to come close enough to walk in on what was going for Huddles. The other way, if it was just the one of us, it would have to be Cathy. It would have to be that someone had plans for her, somebody waiting for a time when he could get her alone.

See what thinking does to a man? I had to hang on to the belief that there would have been two of them, particularly now when I had sent her to the restaurant alone. Work as I would at holding it off, the other thought did keep sneaking around the edges of my mind. I forced myself away from it. I had to because it wouldn't have taken much more before I'd have been beginning to panic.

Pushing myself back to the idea that there had been two of them, I worked up a picture where one had gone off to stow the loot while the other would be keeping the watch. Doing it that way, they would, of course, be taking a chance that just at the time when both of them would be needed Cathy and I would separate and they would lose the one of us.

I could understand the likelihood that they would take that gamble, especially since the stakes had been plenty high enough. The lady, when she left the restaurant, had easily been six figures on the hoof. On my amateur assessment I would have put it at least to edging up on half way to the seven-figure mark. With that much loot right there for the taking and with the fact that Cathy and I had since our first meeting been just about inseparable, it seemed a cinch that one of them would have deserted his post.

On that thinking, if one of them had to keep an eye on the two of us, he must be hanging on somewhere in my vicinity. We had separated, Cathy and I, but she had gone up a dead-end road. She couldn't go anywhere without coming back up to this end and going on out to the highway.

Even though I was comforting myself with that thought, it was with the greatest feeling of relief that I saw Baby bumping over the ruts on her way back to me. Even then I had myself so thoroughly spooked that I caught myself asking God to make it Cathy at the wheel.

It was Cathy, of course, and she didn't question my being all-out glad to see her. It was just as well because I wouldn't have wanted to tell her what I'd been thinking.

It was only a matter of a few minutes before a fuzz-escorted ambulance came screaming down the highway from the town. And that was it. Nothing else came. I left the car and its bloody freight to the fuzz and the medics while I drew Cathy to one side.

"We don't need a crowd," I said, "but it is funny. What goes back at the restaurant? Nobody interested? No accident buffs? Have the people who were through eating started through the menu again?"

"Nobody knows," Cathy said.

"Who called the ambulance?"

Phrase-book Italian over a Sicilian telephone could never have been good enough.

"Oh, the restaurant people. They know. I told the waiter and he told the rest of them. He made the call while all the others ran around like mad busily not giving people the dinner checks they were asking for and busily pushing on everyone after-dinner drinks on the house."

"First law of public feeding," I said. "Bodies are bad for business."

"How is she?"

"Still alive but only just. I don't think she's going to make it."

She didn't. I left Cathy where she was, sitting in the Porsche, and stepped over to talk to the medics and the fuzz. They were working on her but it was obvious that it was a last-ditch effort. I waited while they were making their try. It was no time for creating diversions. Life, Charlie, has to come first. Property, regardless of the quantity, can never run better than a poor second.

After a few minutes the medics came away. But even when we had first come on her, she had already been doing the downward plunge on that last toboggan run. Nobody could have pulled her back out of it. It was probably just as well. There had been far too much damage. If she had lived it would have been for nothing you could call living, a basket case, no more than technically alive.

The fuzz took my statement. They didn't bother Cathy. I told them that anything she had seen I had seen, and she didn't speak Italian.

"When we found them," I said, "he was dead and she— you saw the way she was. We had seen them at dinner and we had seen them leave the restaurant. They left about five minutes before we did, maybe a minute or two more than that. It was very little time, but by the time we got here they had been robbed, and the robbers were nowhere in sight."

"Robbed?"

"She was wearing diamonds. Rings, bracelets, brooches, earrings, all big stones, a great fortune in diamonds. All the jewelry was stripped from her."

That statement brought on a flood of questions. They

were the obvious ones. Between the time they had left the restaurant and the time we pulled out, had any other patrons left?

I had a definite answer to that one and it was negative. They had gone and we had been the next to leave.

"Did any of the restaurant people follow them when they left?"

"Not so far as we could see."

"Waiters? Kitchen help?"

"I can answer for the waiters," I said. "All the waiters we saw were there all the time. They'd go out to the kitchen to leave an order or to pick up, but they were never gone from the dining room for long, never long enough to have come this far down the road, rob the woman, and make it back to the dining room again."

"Kitchen help?"

"We weren't out to the kitchen. We wouldn't know about them."

"We will question them. It is regrettable that we must inconvenience you, but we must ask you to return to the restaurant with us."

Back at the restaurant it was crazy. Nobody but Cathy and I had seen any diamonds at all. The cops worked on all the restaurant staff and they worked on all the patrons in the place. None of them had noticed the couple, much less anything they had been wearing. The waiter who had served them couldn't, of course, pretend that he had taken no notice of them, but he had a glib explanation for his blindness.

"A waiter," he said. "Any waiter who does his job right has too many things to watch, too many things he must keep in mind. He cannot allow his attention to stray to things that are not his business."

The patrons for the most part offered no explanations.

They simply hadn't seen or hadn't taken notice or were simply unable to remember. One of them did explain, and he could have been putting it for all of them.

"A man comes here to eat and to look at the temples," he said. "He looks at his food. He looks at his wine. He looks at the temples because they are beautiful. If he takes his eyes off the temples, it will be to look at his wife because she is beautiful as well. Who would look at diamonds? Diamonds you can see anywhere, in any jewelry store window. Who would come to Agrigento to bother his head about diamonds?"

The answer to that one was left unspoken but it was there, hanging all around me. It would have to be that stock character, the materialistic American, the man who is so obsessed with dollars and cents that he can appreciate nothing unless it will be in terms of what a thing costs.

Of course, I wasn't believing a word of it and no more were the fuzz. I knew the score and so did they. The restaurant people were doing no more than following an age-old Sicilian tradition. Your ordinary, average Sicilian—and he is far from being alone in this attitude—feels that he is always in the middle, caught between the savagery of the criminals and the savagery of the police. The secret of survival is to keep oneself uninvolved. If involvement should be unavoidable, a wise man takes the course that will hold his involvement down to the minimum. If he must tilt toward one side or the other, he tilts toward the criminal for that, too, is the policy of survival.

Justice is a chancy and a sometime thing. Criminal retribution is quick, efficient, and inescapable. A man who can bring himself to rob a dying woman is a savage. Only a fool will open his mouth and invite the hostility of such a savage.

The diners were also following long-established tradition.

If not all the Italians among them were taking the course of Sicilian wisdom, any exceptions would be following the tourist tradition. Even if you are not on one of those schedules that calls for hitting thirteen countries in eleven days, you don't let yourself in for anything that might disrupt your plans. Make yourself a witness to anything, and you may be required to hang around for some indeterminate time to give testimony. This isn't your city and maybe it isn't even your country. Let the locals take care of their local problems. You are only passing through.

When I opened my mouth, I had been aware that I could be putting myself and probably Cathy as well into a situation that would mess up our schedule. It hadn't bugged me any, and maybe because I had no schedule. If we had to hang on in Agrigento for a while, the only one of us who might have been inconvenienced would have been Huddles since he was still holding his point on Taormina. And, I was not at all sure that inconveniencing Huddles had to be a bad thing.

As it turned out, however, we weren't delayed. Nobody wanted Erridge's testimony. It wasn't that the fuzz didn't believe me. It was only that before that evening had run its course, any testimony Erridge might have had to offer had become moot. Evidence turned up that proved me right about the diamonds, but that very same evidence relieved the fuzz of any need for following up on the robbery angle.

As soon as the bodies had been taken away and the *carabinieri* had turned to examining the other stuff in the car, they found locked in the trunk a heavily loaded jewel case. It looked as though every last thing I had seen on the lady was neatly tucked away in that jewel case.

Although you never could have guessed it from seeing her, she had gone into the restaurant, if not half naked, at least underdressed. There was a diamond necklace and a diamond tiara, and she hadn't been wearing either of those. There were also far more rings than any one woman would have finger room for wearing all at one time.

With that much there, it was, of course, not impossible that she could have owned all this plus what we had seen her wearing, but it wasn't likely. Too many of the items were recognizable and nobody was going to assume that she would have owned that many in exact duplicates.

The thing seemed to add up, of course, for a crazy combination of prudence and imprudence. It would have to be that the lady couldn't bear to sit down to dinner without being festooned with at least a good part of her rocks but that at the same time she thought it unwise to ride a dark back road with all that glitter on display.

It would have to be that they had driven up to the restaurant and parked. Before going in, however, they had opened the trunk, brought out the jewel case, and selected the stuff she was going to wear. Sitting in the car, she would have adorned herself and then the case would have been locked away again in the trunk.

After dinner it would have been the process in reverse.

If anybody had asked me, I would have said it was far more dangerous to go through all that routine in a dark parking lot than to go riding along with all the stuff on her. The possibility of a holdup while she was dressing or undressing seemed to me to have been all too good, and if that had happened, the necklace and the tiara and all those surplus rings would have been taken as well.

There was also another item I found peculiar. In her cautious phase she had been all-out cautious. It looked as though she had taken off every last diamond. It could hardly have been otherwise since her diamond-studded wedding band and the huge rock she had worn with it on

the fourth finger of her left hand were in the jewel case with
the rest of the stuff. If a woman has taken off even her wedding ring and engagement ring, she's not likely to have held
back on anything else.

V.

And that was it. The official verdict said there had been no robbery. Although *Signor* Erridge's assistance was much appreciated, the local officialdom was all too obviously relieved at finding itself in a position to declare his information of no consequence.

I couldn't blame them. I would have liked it if I could have been convinced along with them. I just couldn't believe it. I don't know what I could have believed. If the picture as presented made no sense to me, there was no other picture I managed to dream up that made better sense. Let's face it. I couldn't dream up anything that even made as much sense.

In any event, the authorities required nothing more of me and nothing at all of Cathy. We were free to move on any time we chose.

Since Huddles wanted to move, we pulled out the next morning. It was again the cheerful and co-operative new Huddles, but now with a small difference. All through that day's jump, every inch of the way from Agrigento to Siracusa we never once lost the Rolls out of Baby's rear-view mirror.

When we rolled up to our Siracusa hotel, Huddles came in right on our tail. I was just opening my car door when

Huddles planted himself alongside it and pushed it back shut.

"This place looks crummy," he said. "Let's skip it."

I let Cathy have a try at fielding that one.

"It doesn't look crummy to me, and Matt says it's a good town. He says I'm going to like it here."

"Matt says," Huddles grumbled. "Matt says, Matt says, Matt says. I'm not going to like it here. I've seen all I want to see of this place."

"I haven't," Cathy said, holding firm. "Give it a chance, Huddles. You'll see. You'll like it. You liked Selinunte and you loved Agrigento. This is more of the same."

"That's just it, more of the same. I've had a bellyful of more of the same. We can take a break from it in Taormina, and we can come back this way and catch it on the way back."

As far as it went, it was a reasonable suggestion. I could see that Cathy was at a loss for any way of vetoing it that would not go down as nothing more than a stubborn insistence on frustrating him, but I could also see that she did want to veto it. I moved in on the argument and helped her out.

"On the map," I said, "Taormina doesn't look like an impossibly long run, a little more than a hundred kilometers, call it about sixty-five miles."

"Less than two hours," Huddles said. "It's nothing."

"It would be if there was a highway by-pass around Catania, but there isn't and Catania is a big city. It sprawls all over the place, and we'll be fighting city traffic through every inch of it. We'd be hitting it a little after five and that's going to mean the going-home-from-work traffic, and there's a lot of that through a lot of narrow streets. It'll be dark before we're back on the highway."

That was all Cathy wanted. Now she could pick up the ball and run with it.

"And that's the stretch where we'll be seeing Mount Etna. I'm not going to go riding past Mount Etna in the dark and never see it at all."

"You'll see it on the way back."

"Tomorrow by daylight."

She was standing fast, but he wasn't ready to surrender.

"Okay," he said. "I'm going on. I'll see you in Taormina tomorrow."

I felt her go tense beside me. I didn't quite know what this was on his side, but on hers it wasn't just a battle of wills. The kid was scared. If she could have thought of any way she could have fixed it so we wouldn't go to Taormina at all, she would have grabbed at it. She had been yanking at the leash too long and and she knew it.

Huddles was in full rebellion. Nothing was going to keep him away from Taormina. It was only a question of whether he would be going there alone or we would be there as well. I was wondering what she thought we could do if we were there. Catch him when he fell? Had they been through this other times? Were there signs she knew how to read?

Whichever way it was for her, there were the signs I knew how to read. She was not going to let him go on to Taormina alone. If necessary, we would skip this Siracusa stop and go on with him, but she didn't want to do that. It was at times like these, in just these moments when he came down with a special urgency to go to Taormina and without delay that she seemed to be most eager to hold him back.

The way I was reading it, she was thinking that these sudden bouts of urgency had to mean that he would have something going for him in Taormina then and not later and that maybe, if she could make him be late for it, it could be that he would have missed the boat completely and would be out of danger. Of that one thing I was certain. It was no question of moral scruples that was eating on her. She was frightened for him, and she was frightened of some physical danger.

I couldn't help thinking that the poor kid was beating herself up for nothing. Her Huddles was a big boy and with his tastes and his proclivities and with the kind of company he evidently liked to keep he was going to take a bad fall sooner or later, and there would be nothing she could do to prevent it or even to soften its effects. I was also thinking that maybe if she didn't stand by to catch him when he fell, he might even learn how to take care of himself.

Whatever I was thinking, however, I could feel that for her everything was riding on the one thing, keeping him out of Taormina that night. Whether she was right or wrong, I couldn't let her be wanting anything that much and do nothing to get it for her.

Argument was going to be no good. I thought wildly of a clip on the chin that would knock him cold. Then we could tie him hand and foot and carry him into the hotel to hold him prisoner till morning.

I didn't think she would go for that. I was pretty certain that no hotel would go for it, not the one we were parked at and not any other anywhere. How can a guest sign a registration card if he is tied hand and foot? I knew that I didn't go for it. It may be a way of influencing people, but it's no way to make friends or to keep the ones you've made. I did want to keep Cathy.

When opposition won't get you anywhere, there's nothing you can do but try agreement. I took his suggestion as though it were a great idea. I was all co-operation. Carefully avoiding Cathy's eye—I knew she was reading me for treachery—I set about being Huddles' ally and helper.

"The highway into Catania is no problem," I said. "There are no side roads you could stray into by mistake and get yourself lost. You just stay with the highway and you'll have no problems. Anyhow, it's well marked all the way. After you're out of Catania, you have the same easy highway situation on to Taormina. Nothing can be easier even if you are doing it in the dark."

"I'll be okay."

Huddles didn't want to stop for any talk. He was itching to be on the road. Taormina was calling and the summons seemed to be more urgent than it had ever been before.

"The tricky part," I continued, "is getting through Catania. Once you're in the city there are very few highway markers, and the few there are you'd be better off without. They're only confusing."

I fed him street-by-street, turning-by-turning instructions on the route through the city. I didn't have to exaggerate the confusion. It's there. You'd have to search hard through all of Italy to find a drearier city than Catania. You get to wondering why anyone would want to live there, but before you've found your way out of the place, you know. It's not that anyone wants to live there. It's just that people have driven in and have never been able to find their way out.

Maybe I could have made it a little less confusing. I'm not at all certain that it would have been possible, but I'll never know because I didn't try. Since I honestly could not remember all the street names, the instructions I was giving him were obviously hopeless.

You know that deal where you'll recognize a turning when you come to it but for the life of you can't remember whether it's the third intersection after the second traffic light or the second intersection after the third light.

I went through it with him again and again, and on each repetition I had him more befuddled. He was developing that glazed look and he was reaching the place where he was no longer able to follow even those simpler parts of it that he had been following all right the first time through.

Cathy—she's a bright little peachcake—began to see what I was building. Waiting till we'd reached a moment of impasse, she jumped in and helped.

"After all," she said, "if you get hopelessly lost in Catania, you can always go to a hotel there and try again tomorrow."

"Tomorrow?"

Huddles repeated the word after her. He sounded as though he were talking out of a stupor.

Cathy brightened. She'd had a great idea.

"If you do have to go to a hotel in Catania," she said, "you can call us here. Just remember the name of this hotel. Then tomorrow on our way through, we'll stop by your hotel and Matt can lead you out to the highway."

Huddles sighed. He knew when he was licked. A night in Catania was not what he wanted. All the same, his complete surrender took me by surprise. I had hoped only that, trying to follow my directions, he would get so hopelessly lost in Catania that Cathy would have at least that part of what she wanted. He would have been delayed that one day in getting to Taormina.

"I'll wait till tomorrow," he growled.

So I'd succeeded, but it wasn't long before I was wishing I hadn't. We were right back to the Segesta Huddles, determined that he would hate everything and enjoy nothing and equally set on spoiling it for Cathy. This was the town where Archimedes lived and died and where Alcibiades fell on his ass. In the theater here Aechylus got his first performance of *The Persians*. Huddles tagged along after us.

He did everything. He looked at everything and at every turn he muttered, "Who cares?"

When we hit the Zona Archeologica, he brightened. You think the ancient Greek ruins grabbed him once he gave them the chance? Think again. The modern city has grown out around the ruin area. They've made a park of the zone. It's grass and trees and shrubs and winding paths with a surprise around almost every turn.

We were no sooner inside the gate than Huddles was off and winging, and I knew what he was hoping to find. In the Zona Archeologica at Segesta he'd found the man who needed a light or the man had found him. On the road into Agrigento he had fallen back and arrived an hour late and bubbling over with good spirits.

He obviously had found someone on the road or someone had found him. In Agrigento everything had been great and then abruptly that last night it had gone sour for him and he was back to the way he had been when we'd first started out of Palermo. I couldn't work out any reasonable basis for the thought that kept coming at me, but, reasonable or not, it did keep coming at me. Could there have been any connection between that fatal accident on the road from the restaurant and this sudden change that had come over Huddles?

On the way I'd been reading it until the fuzz had come up with the jewel case, excellent reasons presented themselves. These people he was playing around with were obviously a bad lot. If it had been that one or more of them had been watching at the end of that road, keeping an eye on Cathy and me, and the opportunity for the big jewel heist had presented itself, then it would work out.

They would have grabbed the diamonds and have made the immediate pull-out from Agrigento. I'd been thinking in terms of some kind of gang operation and I could imagine the whole gang lamming out of there, suddenly leaving Huddles high and dry.

Taking it that way, I could see how he would have shifted to wanting to be on the move again. As there had been the contact at Segesta and another on the road into Agrigento, he had been hoping for a fresh contact along the Agrigento-Siracusa road.

Disappointed of that, he had been hell bent on skipping this Siracusa stop. He was out of contact and Taormina would have seemed his best bet for re-establishing contact, but now in the Siracusa archeological zone he was suddenly hopeful again.

Along those winding paths, in one or another of those leafy nooks and crannies, he could have every hope of coming on a messenger or of a messenger coming on him. Why would it not be as it had been at Segesta or on the road into Agrigento? All he might have to do is separate himself from Cathy and me.

It made sense all the way, or it would have except for the one thing. The fuzz had found the jewel case. My robbery idea was down the drain. At the beginning, when the police had checked the dead man's pockets and found so much money on him, my theory hadn't been knocked out. It hadn't even been jolted. On a quick grab-and-run job with that great haul of loot out in plain sight, they wouldn't have stopped to go checking into pockets.

One didn't need to be thinking that there was a limit to their greed. There was a limit, of course, but it was on the time they had for grabbing what they could and making a safe getaway. We would have been coming down on them and they would have had ample warning. From that far end of the road they would have seen Baby's lights and they would have seen me swing her out of the restaurant parking

lot and start her down the dirt road in the only direction
there was to go, straight toward them.

All this was great thinking, but then there was the evidence, and the evidence said it had been happening nowhere but inside Erridge's head. I could see no way of getting around that jewel case. Those diamonds weren't
theory, they were a fact. I've always figured myself for
being a practical, clear-eyed, down-to-earth, realist. Only a
fool is going to fight the facts, but that jewel case was a fact
I could find no way of believing.

Women, and particularly older women, so far as I knew
them, usually had a special thing about wedding rings.
Whether it was superstition or sentiment, they didn't take
them off. Could this have been a woman who was immune
to both superstition and sentiment? That would make her
an unconventional, enlightened type, and I was remembering her the way she had been at dinner. I would have said
she was anything else but.

Peculiar or not, however, there it was—no robbery. All
my doubts, all my gut feelings, and all my searching around
brought me no other answer.

For most of what was left of the afternoon I wandered
the ruins with Cathy. If you're ever in that part of the
world, you might want to remember it. It's a great place to
take a girl. Those winding paths, those nooks and crannies,
you can't ask for better when you want that whole-world-
to-yourselves feeling. Adam and Eve before they were
booted out of the garden. Erridge and Cathy among the
ruins. Huddles and some guy who would need a light?

I put him out of my mind and maybe Cathy forgot him,
too, at least for a little while. I like to think she did. A couple of times our paths crossed and each time he was alone.
Each time, furthermore, he looked more sulky and more
sour. The last time he had come looking for us.

"I've had a bellyfull of this," he said. "You can have it."

Cathy slipped out of character.

"Where are you going?" she asked.

Mostly she was careful not to question him. He was quick to remind her of that.

"Do I ask you?" he said.

"Sorry."

He turned to me.

"Early start tomorrow morning?"

"We're in no hurry."

"I am. I'm in one hell of a hurry."

"Okay. Then as soon as Cathy is ready to go."

He scowled.

"Leave it to her and she'll have to wash her hair and paint her toenails, and she'll shop for something she suddenly can't do without and it'll be something you can't ever find in all of Sicily. Something like a hula skirt or a Houston Oilers T-shirt."

Cathy took the sarcasm and rolled with it.

"I don't know how early I'll be ready in the morning," she said. "It depends on how big a night we'll be having. I want dinner in the old city and after dinner a *bottegha* binge. Matt says the old city is a swinging place."

Huddles looked doubtful.

"Old city?" he mumbled. "Older than this?"

"Ancient city, old city, and modern city," I explained. "It's medieval and renaissance, older than the modern city and not as old as this Greek stuff."

"It jumps?"

"It's where the night life is."

He brightened in spite of himself.

"All right," he said, "but push yourself a little. Make it early tomorrow."

He was still grumbling but it was beginning to sound like

a forced grumble. There was a lot of optimism in that lad. Since he had drawn a blank along the winding paths, he was off to try his luck in the old city.

Cathy gave him one of her best smiles.

"I'll try, Huddles. That's a promise."

He smiled back at her. He had a good smile. After all, it was too much like hers to be anything else.

"A promise, Cuddles," he said. "Don't forget."

"Do I ever forget?"

"No. You don't."

He kissed her cheek.

They had moments like that, and when they would, I'd get to feeling as though I wasn't even there. I don't think that either of them ever set out deliberately to remind me that come what may I was and always would be an outsider.

It wasn't any big night, not for Cathy and me, and, as far as I could tell, not for Huddles. We wandered the old town. We had dinner. We sat out in front of cafes in one little square after another and we drank a little wine. Now and again we caught a glimpse of Huddles. Down a dark side street we passed a crowded little bar and we saw him in there. It was obvious that he was buying and that could have been the reason why the place was so crowded. It didn't look like a particularly good bar. We met him again and he was walking alone. He just waved in passing. He looked sad and lost, but he obviously didn't want to join up with us.

The hotel sent up a morning paper with my breakfast. It was the local rag. Most of what they print in those provincial dailies may be news to the people who live in the place, but it's nothing that can mean much to an outsider. They do, however, carry one or two national or international items. It's worth glancing at over the rolls, butter, jam, honey, and coffee. In case the world came to an end while you weren't looking, they'd let you know.

As soon as I'd picked it up, the Page 1 picture caught my eye. It was a gruesome shot. Even without color printing the blood jumped out at you. More to the point, it was a shot I recognized—I had been there when it was being taken. It was picture of that smashup back in Agrigento, the wrecked car complete with its wrecked occupants.

An accident and two people dead—okay, it's a story and a good, gory picture like that might be irresistible in any editorial league, but it had happened in another town. At first jump I could think of only one explanation for so big a play and that would be that the couple had been celebrities. He could have been an olive-oil or tomato-paste king. She could have been the madam of Milan's busiest house.

Out of curiosity I read the headline.

THE ROBBERY THAT WASN'T.

I was hooked. I had to settle in and read every word. It was going to be a funny story, within the limits, of course, to which sudden death can be funny. I expected that it would be a tale of how this stupid American had yelled robbery on nothing more than the slim grounds that the fat lady had made an early start on undressing for bed. I don't know that I was ready to join in the laughter, but you do have to look if only to see whether they've spelled your name right.

So I read it and I was wrong. They had not only spelled Erridge right but they also made Erridge out to be something of a hero, the one honest man in a nest of the mendacious. Erridge had seen the lady encrusted with her diamonds. Erridge had seen the lady stripped of her rocks. Erridge had yelled robbery and Erridge had been right. Despite the fact that not one diamond had been taken, Erridge had been right.

They played with the contradiction as long as they could, telling the story step by step and leaving the zinger to explode in the reader's face at the last.

There had been other luggage in that car trunk along with the jewel case and in one of the suitcases the police had come upon the perfect replicas of the diadem, the necklace, and several rings and bracelets, replicas of all those of the lady's jewels that the admirably observant American signor had not seen on the lady's person.

The replicas were exact but only to the naked and unprofessional eye. The diamonds in the jewel case were diamonds and all choice stones of the greatest value. The duplicates in the suitcase were only paste replicas, phonies the lady wore when, despite her fears for the safety of the costly originals, she couldn't endure the thought of appearing in public in a state of nakedness.

So it was a gleeful story, resounding with the triumphant chuckles of the righteous. The lowest of animals in human form had committed this ghoulish crime and it was availing him nothing. In the evident hope that this lowest animal was also a newspaper reader, the story worked at rubbing it in.

It expanded on the horde that had been locked away in the car trunk. It went to great length in explaining that the trunk lock had been no obstacle. The force of the crash had sprung the lock. How much easier and quicker it could have been to reach into the gaping car trunk and lift out the jewel case than to rip each piece from her one by one and gather in the full harvest of fakes.

That, furthermore, was not all of the story's gloating. The ghoul had been so heavily engaged in gathering in all those phonies from the body of the dying woman that he hadn't so much as touched the dead man. He'd made off with his haul of trash and he had left behind the great roll of lira the man had in his pocket and the even greater rolls of that negotiable stuff he'd had cinched around him in a money belt.

With obvious regret the story did concede that the ghoul had not come away from his venture with a totally non-profit haul. All those paste replicas had been set in gold. With gold bringing record prices, it was estimated that the settings would bring a not inconsiderable sum; but, in comparison with what he'd thought he had, it would be no more than the most miserable pittance.

For me, however, that story carried a lot more meaning than the reporter could have dreamed he was putting into it. My whole sequence of theories that had fallen on its face without the robbery to give it a foundation was now standing solid and it was demanding attention.

Huddles' playmates had been luring him to Taormina where they had been planning to take him and take him but good. Because we had been dragging him around on the archeological route they had been forced to postpone their Taormina deal, but these were flexible men. They had been riding along with it, following us around and keeping Huddles in play.

In Agrigento serendipity had taken over. The part of the band that had been watching us while the rest had been engaged in keeping Huddles happy and safely on the hook, had fallen into what looked like a record-breaking haul of diamonds. So then it was first things first. No time to be bothered with keeping Huddles happy when they had all those diamonds to transport to some far-off place where they could be safely and profitably fenced.

Maybe they had been planning to pick up on him again when they had dealt with this new business that had come to hand. Maybe they had seen no way of doing both, and with a choice of one or the other, they had taken the obvious course. Take no unnecessary chances. Cash in on what you already have in the bag.

Given the news, it was easy to understand the abrupt overnight change in Agrigento. All of a sudden the fun had stopped. All of a sudden there was nobody around to keep Huddles happy. Nobody to set up fun and games in Siracusa. Everything fitted. Everything dovetailed.

And now the game would go on. I could assume that by now they knew what they had. If they hadn't already learned it, this newspaper story would have told them. They would be in Taormina with their appetites whetted to a keener than ever edge. The way I saw it, this was going to cost Huddles and cost him plenty; and I must admit it, I couldn't have cared less.

I was seeing it as nothing more than nature's way of keeping something going in the way of distributing the wealth. A family goes on for any number of generations raking it in and piling it up until it's way past the place where it's far too much. At that point the right little genes meet up and they produce a Cuddles and a Huddles, and at least some of the amassed bread gets spread around.

Back in Naples that first morning it hadn't happened but only because Erridge spoiled that relatively small rip-off. Just on the time and the effort that had been put into it, what was waiting for Huddles in Taormina had to be the big rip-off, and I was seeing no way that Erridge could step into that one and do anybody any good.

You can be thinking that I was seeing no way because I was content to let it happen, and it could be that you're right. I thought it was going to be only money and, since in that area the wombmates couldn't have cared less, why should I have worked up a sweat about it?

When Huddles came knocking at my door, I had to figure that even though it was still early, he was in such a sweat to be on the road to Taormina that he couldn't even wait till I came downstairs. The only other possibility I could see was that Cathy had actually been up by crack of dawn and had already come down so that everything was waiting on slug-a-bed Erridge.

Both possibilites made sense though I was inclined to favor the first one. I was wrong on both. Huddles wasn't openly impatient, but he wasn't exactly relaxed. He was just working on looking loose and easy.

"Cathy down already?" I asked.

"This early? You've got to be kidding."

"We can't move till she's ready."

"I know that. I'm not pushing. Tell me, Matt. What's in Taormina?"

"Sun, swimming, scenery. Mount Etna in the distance."

"How would it be if we skipped it?"

I've never been known to be slow on the uptake, but I did need a little while before that could percolate.

"Taormina's been your bag, Hughie boy. It never was mine."

"I know. And not Cathy's either. I got to thinking last night. If Taormina is what I think it is, and now you say it is just that, then it hasn't anything Sardinia hasn't got, and our crowd is all up there in Sardinia and it's where Cuddles wanted to go."

"You've known that all along," I reminded him.

He put on a rueful-little-boy look.

"I know," he said. "I'm like that. I get these silly stubborn moods and, until I'm over them, I'm the world's prime pain in the ass. I know I've been a pain, Matt, and I'm sorry. I made you guys rush out of Palermo when Cuddles wanted to stay and see it. I want to make it up to her."

I couldn't remember Cathy as having wanted to hang on in Palermo. The argument hadn't been about heading south. It had been about the route we would take. I let the difference pass.

"We'll take some Palermo time on our way back to the mainland," I said.

"I know, but that's the way we've had it set up all along. I've been beastly to Cuddles ever since Naples, and I want to make it up to her—I want to really show her I'm sorry. I want to give up something just to please her. I want to give up Taormina."

"We can take it up with her," I said.

I was reading him like a book. During the night he'd gotten the word. Either the Taormina deal was completely off or else it had been transferred to Palermo. I thought the latter more likely. Taormina is a small place where there's no business but resort business. Palermo is a city, a much more likely place to go if you have hot diamonds to fence, or if you want to get lost in a crowd. The gang had moved up to Palermo and during the night in the old city they had made contact and invited Huddles up there to get fleeced.

We went downstairs together. Huddles was happy as a lark. Since I wasn't opposing him, he was confident that Cathy would put nothing in the way of his valiant effort.

And he wasn't wrong. Cathy had been too long focussed on Taormina. She had come to dread it as a danger spot. Suddenly relieved of any necessity for going there, she was not about to ask any questions. So far as she was concerned, Huddles was like that, and if this time he was cured of his dangerous obsession before anything happened, she was not going to knock it.

With surface harmony never more complete we pulled out of Siracusa. We were only a few miles down the highway when he began dropping back. It was a crazy time for that caper because we were coming up on the Catania headache, and he knew he was going to need me to lead him through the city to the Catania-Palermo *autostrada*. I slowed Baby down and we cruised along, giving him every opportunity to catch up with us.

Then it was only a few minutes, not more than three or four kilometers farther on, when the Rolls turned up again in my rearview mirror. It hung there all the rest of the way into Catania and in the city streets it sat close on my tail. We had lunch in Catania and shoved on right after eating. All through lunch Huddles was gay and happy and full of fun. He kept Cathy laughing. He had me even beginning to like him.

The rest of the way through the tangle of city streets he was again no problem. Once we were on the highway, however, he again dropped back. I thought it would be as it had been in the morning, a matter of only a few minutes. When the minutes had stretched into an hour, I switched to thinking it was going to be as it had been on the way into Agrigento. He wasn't going to catch up at all. He'd just come cruising into the Palermo hotel an hour or two after we got there.

We got there. An hour passed and the second. The third hour had all but run out before anything came, and then it wasn't the Rolls and it wasn't Huddles. It was the ransom demand.

VI.

"Right now he is safe. He will be returned alive on payment of three million dollars. Delay payment and he will suffer terrible agony. Stay by telephone for payment instructions. Do not enlist police. If there is any police interference, Mr. Hugh Martin will be killed."

That was the message. It was made up of individual words and phrases clipped out of an English-language newspaper and pasted down on a sheet of paper to piece together the sentences. The envelope was similarly addressed. It had nothing on it but a pasted on bit of printed matter that read: "Miss Catherine Martin." There was no address. None had been needed. The envelope had been left at the hotel desk by a messenger.

The two names, each complete in a single piece, were not, like the rest of it, on ordinary newsprint. They were on glossy stock, evidently clipped out of a picture caption in one of those magazines that chronicle the movements of the beautiful people.

I was with her when the desk clerk handed her the message. We were on our way out to dinner. The clerk said it had been delivered only a few moments before. He had been on the point of sending it up to her room.

She ripped it open and read it. I saw her eyes widen and

the color drain from her face, but she stood steady. She tried to speak. It was no go. For the moment she couldn't find her voice. Silently she held the message out for me to take it. In taking it, I touched her hand. Her fingers had gone icy cold but her hand wasn't shaking.

I read it through and turned to the desk clerk.

"Did you see the man who brought this?"

"A messenger."

He'd said only a few moments. That Palermo hotel sits in the middle of a great expanse of lawn and garden with the entrance to the hotel property at the end of a road that leads to nothing but the hotels grounds. The speediest messenger would need more than a few moments to get himself down the hotel driveway and out to the road. He would need even longer before he could go the length of that road that would take him out to a street where he might lose himself in a crowd or might go to earth in any one of a lot of buildings.

I grabbed at the clerk's arm.

"You'll know the man," I said. "I want him before he gets away from here."

I thought there would be every chance of it but not, of course, if we didn't move and move fast. We didn't move.

"Know him?" the clerk said. "Just a bum with a dirty face. Palermo is full of such bums."

"Come on anyhow. We can give it a try."

Then Cathy found her voice. She dropped her hand on my arm, holding me.

"No, Matt," she said. "I'll pay it. I don't want him hurt. Not for money, not for anything."

Thinking I had no time to stop for argument, I tried a quick end run around her reluctance.

"You can tell that to the messenger and get the word to his kidnappers quicker, if that's the way you want it."

It was the right approach. It worked. She squeezed my arm and then quickly pulled her restraining hand away.

The clerk wasn't that easy.

"I don't think I'll know him," he said. "I didn't take any notice of him. We don't like bums here in the lobby. We don't take time to look at them. We just get rid of them as quick as we can."

"We're giving it a try."

I wasn't asking for any favor. I was snapping out a command.

The clerk called an assistant and told him to take over on the desk. On his way around from behind his counter, he paused to give his temporary replacement about a dozen instructions. The assistant wasn't a quick study. Some of the instructions had to be repeated.

"You're not going away for a month," I growled. "You'll be back in a minute."

He broke loose but there was no hurrying him.

"We're not going to find him," he said. "It's been too long."

"It will be the way you're moving."

"No. It's already been too long. Fifteen minutes and more."

"You said only a moment or two."

The clerk shrugged.

"Just a way of speaking," he said. "I was going to send it upstairs just as soon as I had a bellboy free."

I tried anyway. The Porsche was parked handy because we had been going to use her to go to dinner. When the clerk realized that he was to have a ride in Baby, his attitude changed. He began to think that maybe he would recognize the bum.

We covered the whole area, the full length of the hotel driveway, the full length of the dead-end road. All the way we saw nobody. At the end of the road where it opened into the city streets we hit a roaring stream of traffic and a swarming eddy of pedestrians. The messenger was off and gone. The clerk's moment-or-two fifteen minutes had been more than long enough.

Cathy took hold.

"Please, Matt," she said. "Take me back to the hotel."

I got Baby turned around and started back.

"I'm going to order dinner in my room," she said. "I'd like to order for two. You'll eat with me, Matt?"

"Of course."

"Thanks. First thing I must call New York to get the money made available here."

"That much just like that?" I asked.

She nudged me and shook her head.

I got the message. We had the clerk still with us and she was shutting me up before I might give out with any words like kidnap or ransom. She didn't want him to know or even to be making any guesses. The message hadn't instructed her that she must tell nobody, but she was following even those instructions that hadn't been given her. She wanted to keep this was not only from the police but from anyone who might leak any hint of it to the police.

I waited till I was alone with her in her sitting room. Of course, she had a suite. She always had a suite unless it was a hotel that didn't have any. Traveling with Martins you had to try to avoid such hotels. Confined to any one room, Martins went claustrophobic. Looking around at the acreage Cathy had commanded for herself, I had to wonder how Huddles might be doing in the kidnapper-supplied quarters he was then occupying. Despite the grim suggestions of the note, I had a feeling that of the two of them it would be Cathy who was having the worse time.

The way all the preliminaries had gone, it seemed not

too unlikely that Huddles was the happy captive, so dizzily engaged in a round of pleasures that he wouldn't even know he was being held captive.

He could be having a ball, and if he happened to notice the security arrangements, to him they could appear to be nothing more than what was needed to keep Cathy and me from barging in and spoiling the fun.

It could be so simple for those bastards who had him. To him they would be presenting themselves as buddies dedicated to nothing but keeping his pleasure supply going. Then when the party was over, they would collect the ransom and he wouldn't know that it had been demanded or that it had been paid until they were well gone and he had rejoined us.

I wondered how he was going to be feeling about it then, whether what he was getting would be worth three million bucks to him. I also wondered how he was going to feel about the other cost—what this was doing to Cathy.

"It's your money and your business," I told her. "But if you're smart, you'll let me take that crazy message to the police."

"No."

"Why not?"

"They say they'll torture him and kill him."

She was already on the telephone asking the operator to get her New York. She wasn't long. Within a few moments she came away from the phone, and now she wasn't only white-lipped. She was shaking.

"Circuits are loaded and you'll have to wait?"

She nodded.

"They'll call me as soon as they can get through."

"Don't let the delay bug you. Nobody's so crazy that they'll expect you to come up with three million in cash out of any roll you keep stuffed in the top of your stocking.

These guys have been following us around and watching us all the time they've been building this. They know by now that you don't even wear stockings."

"Please, Matt. I know you're trying to make me feel better, but don't make jokes. I'm scared. If I can't get through to New York for hours and hours and hours, they'll think I'm stalling. I'm scared of what they'll do to Huddles."

I fed her my party-for-him-ransom-message-for-her idea. I couldn't get her to buy it.

"It can't be those people he's been playing around with," she argued. "He'd know them. He could give their descriptions to the police afterward. It has to be people he doesn't know. They grabbed him from behind and they blindfolded him and they'll never let him see their faces. It's not like with a kidnapped baby who wouldn't know people and who couldn't talk."

"People he knows can grab him from behind and blindfold him and keep him that way. He never realizes they were anyone he knew."

"No," she said. "He'd recognize voices or something. These people don't take that kind of chance. Can't it be, Matt, that it's other people, people who saw the kind of places he was going, places where they could get their hands on him, so they stepped in and they did it? People he never knew, Matt? People he couldn't identify afterward? Can't it be that way, Matt?"

It may look as though she was arguing with me, but she wasn't. She was begging me to help her believe what she wanted to believe, this thing that she felt she had to believe if she was going to stand up to what she thought she was going to have to do.

"It can," I said. "Anything is possible, but everything that's happened points the other way. Ever since Naples when they sucked him into coming to Sicily, they were working on just one thing and that was to get him onto the Palermo-Catania *autostrada*. They dropped back far enough behind us so we wouldn't see it when they came in and took him."

"They were trying to get him to Taormina."

"That's what they were telling him, but first it was getting him to want to zip down from Palermo to Taormina by the shortest and quickest route and that meant the Palermo-Catania *autostrada*. But we went the other way and they followed us around with all kinds of chances to take him. With all those chances they never did. Why?"

"Because it's not these people. All they were doing was giving him what he wanted and for a good price. This is different."

"They were doing that in Naples, they didn't have to suck him into coming over here, if it was only for that. They didn't take him before because there was only the one place they could handle it, and that was somewhere on the *autostrada* between here and Catania. Somewhere within easy reach of that *autostrada* they had their prepared hideaway."

Every word I was saying seemed to be added torment for her. She was searching her mind for some way she could break my argument down.

"Then why all that about Taormina? Why didn't they tell him there'd be a great party going in Catania?"

"Because Taormina is the party place. Taormina was salable. You've seen Catania. Fun in Catania? They'd have a hard time making anyone believe that."

"But they couldn't be sure they'd get him onto that road. Selling him Taormina, how could they know you'd take us by the Naples-Palermo ferry? We could just as easily have taken the Naples-Catania ferry and had only the short run over to Taormina without ever touching that *autostrada* up

to Palermo. We could also have driven all the way down to
Reggio Calabria and come over to Sicily on the ferry to
Messina. That would have been another short run to Taor-
mina and miles away from that damn *autostrada*."

"They couldn't be sure," I said, "but they knew how to
handle it. Look at the way they did handle it. Back in
Naples they didn't tell him Taormina. They just told him
Sicily. Any way we came, they were going to pick him up
and party him around in one place after another till they
had him somewhere where the next jump would put him
where they wanted him. When we came by way of
Palermo, they thought we were making it easy for them.
All they had to do was tell him that Taormina was the
party town and he was to hurry right down there. We
spoiled that by insisting on going the long way around."

"But, Matt, something happened the night before we left
Agrigento. They still had him going to Taormina, but all of
a sudden in a great new hurry. Then the next night in
Siracusa something else happened. They switched him off
Taormina and headed him up here."

"That night in Agrigento they didn't have him going anywhere. They ran out on him. He'd lost them and he was in
that panic rush to push straight through to Taormina because it was the only place he could think of where he
might find them again."

"Why would they do that, Matt? How do you know?"

"Cathy, kid, I don't know, but it's the only way I can
make any sense of this whole thing. They ran out on him in
Agrigento because suddenly they had other fish to fry, and
also suddenly they were hot. Remember the people in the
car smashup? The robbery?"

"But there was no robbery. She had all her junk in the
jewel case."

"She had all her junk on her. The real thing she had in the jewel case."

I gave her a rundown on the newspaper story and showed her how at each step it was a neat fit to Huddles' changes of mood and direction.

"The robbery fell into their laps and they couldn't resist it," I explained. "But then they had to get out of town and quick, even at the risk of losing Huddles."

"Even if they had been the real diamonds, I don't think it would have come to what they're asking for Huddles."

I agreed.

"Particularly selling them as they would have to sell them it would come to a lot less. I suppose they grabbed them without thinking it out. There would have been no time for making careful appraisals and estimates."

She groaned.

"And," she said, "they knew they had Huddles so hooked that they could be sure they wouldn't lose him. They were just going to pick him up later whenever and wherever they were going to be ready."

She was obviously right about that. They had picked him up again and easily enough.

"Yes," I said. "They were thinking they could have both but, even if not, at that point they were stuck with the jewelry and they had every reason to think that would be a great haul. So, even if they did lose Huddles, they wouldn't be doing badly and they would have scored at far less risk."

The rest followed simply enough. They found out that they didn't have any diamonds, and, immediately the kidnapping was on again. Sometime during the night they caught up with Huddles in the old city at Siracusa. They told him the Taormina party had folded and the action had moved to Palermo. They probably also had told him that he'd better get up to Palermo quickly before he missed the fun there as well.

By the time I had finished lining it out for her, she was crying. I made no try at stopping her. She needed it. She had been keeping too tight a hold on herself. Need it or not, however, she didn't let herself go on with it. I had put my arms around her and I was holding her close, thinking she could have a good cry all over my shirt front and empty herself of a lot of tensions.

No more than a minute or two after I stopped talking, she pulled away from me, blew her nose, and wiped her eyes. Biting hard on her lip, she forced herself back under control.

"Matt," she said, "if they haven't killed him, they're going to do it. If we're not too late already, what can we do to stop them?"

"Call the police in."

"And make it a certainty? No."

"You're the one who's sure it's a certainty either way you handle it."

"There has to be another way. I'll give them the money but what else can I do? How can I convince them that there will be nothing afterward? Huddles won't identify them."

"You can promise them that you won't even let it be known that there ever was a kidnapping, that the police will never come into it at all. They might believe you. I don't know."

Her eyes were fixed on the telephone. I think she was trying to hypnotize it into ringing.

"I could promise them that," she said, "but I don't know that I could make it sound convincing. I'd be lying."

"You mean that you couldn't promise for Huddles?" I asked.

"No," she said. "It isn't Huddles. It's the trustees. You

see, we haven't any money, Huddles and I. It's all trust funds. We get only the income and we always get all of that spent. Out of income available now I couldn't possibly scrape together anything like three million dollars. The trustees are going to have to lend it to me out of future income or take it out of principle or something like that."

"And something like that is what trustees won't ever do unless they know what you need all that money for."

"That's the way trustees are," she said. "Of course, it's the way Puddles wanted them to be. That was why the trust funds. He knew how silly we were about money. He knew because he was almost as silly about it himself. He explained the whole thing to us. His father had known all about money, how to make it, how to keep it, how to make it grow, and all that. He'd done everything he knew how to teach Puddles, and not much of it took. As far back as Puddles could remember, when he was a little boy he never had an allowance. He had to do all sorts of crazy chores to earn a couple of dollars, and then he was expected to give an accounting of where every penny of that went. Spending any of it at all meant a lecture on thrift. Admitting that he'd spent anything on something grandfather disapproved meant a whipping. Any time he wasn't able to account for even a penny of it, it would be a worse whipping."

"And he ended up silly about money?"

"Not completely idiotic like Huddles and me. He thought if he did it the other way, let us have money to spend, we'd learn how to handle it, and anyhow there wasn't any other way he could have done it. Whip either of us? He could never have done that. He wasn't that kind of a man. He was a darling."

"But his way didn't work any better than his father's had?"

"Worse. He knew enough to set up the trust funds. We're idiots."

I was keeping her going because I hoped talking would relax her and I might be able to get her to make sense.

I did get a picture, however, of the vise she was in. If the kidnapper was impatient, there would be a question about how long he could be persuaded to wait. To me it seemed a serious question. To her, with her certainty that no matter how things went, her twin brother was going to be killed, her concern was without logic. If, as she kept insisting, he was already dead—or in any case irrevocably slated for death—it could hardly matter much if his kidnappers were to be irritated by delay.

At first I'd thought that her conviction of no hope of ever again seeing him alive had to be simple hysteria. Listening to her go on about it, though, I came down with an uncomfortable feeling that this could be an area where she knew more of the facts of life than I did. I hadn't spent all my life running around with the kidnapee set and she had.

Among her friends she had known families that had met every ransom demand and had followed every detail of the kidnapper's instructions and for all their money and all their pains had come up with nothing in the end but a corpse, and in some cases not even that. She was speaking out of her own knowledge. That was the hard basis of her agonized certainty.

At the same time, however, the thought was too terrible. She couldn't live with it. She had to keep trying to push it away. A way for doing that was to assume the possibility of what she considered would be a miracle. Somehow, in some inconceivable fashion, Huddles could be saved; but if he couldn't, it would have to be because it had always been inevitable, not because she had done anything wrong or had permitted the making of any wrong moves.

Thinking at that level, she could agonize over the delay in getting through to New York. As long as she could pretend to herself that it might make a difference, she could put off facing up fully to what in her heart she felt to be the fact.

Although I was hardly as hopelessly certain as she was, she did have me almost convinced, and brutal as I would have to be, I could see no better possibility of convincing her than by talking and acting as though I were totally convinced.

"Somebody's going to call you here and give you instructions," I said. "When he makes that call, he will be giving you an advantage. You've got to take it."

"An advantage? How?"

"You're in a hotel. You're not in any place of your own. There's no direct telephone line. He has to get the switchboard downstairs and ask to be connected to you up here. That always takes a little time. In Italy, more often than not, it takes a lot of time. Given enough time, the telephone company can pin down the location from which the call is being made. Mostly they aren't successful because a smart criminal keeps the call too short; but with the added time of switchboard handling, you're in a position to prolong it without rousing any suspicion."

She was interested. For a moment she even seemed to be entertaining some spark of hope.

"Can you get the telephone people to do it without telling them why or letting them guess?"

"No," I said. "We'd have to do it through the police. It means bringing them in and the phone company and the hotel. The police will probably want to put one of their own people on the switchboard, someone who'll know how to keep things hung up in one delay after another so that the phone people will have all the time they need."

Long before I had gone through all of that, she had stopped listening. Her look of hope closed down and she was shaking her head.

"It's no good," she said. "We can't do it."

"Why not?"

"You know what they said they'd do if I bring in the police."

"They say they'll kill him," I told her, using the word she was trying not to speak and not to hear. "You're convinced that they'll kill him whatever you do. This way there's a chance of getting to him before they kill him. The other way is just giving up. There's everything to gain and nothing to lose. They can't kill him twice."

"I can make them angry and they'll take it out on him. They can torture him to death. They've as good as threatened that."

"Whatever you do or whatever you don't do, there's some risk."

"I know, Matt. Don't think I don't know, but I can't do it."

It was no good. I had to drop it and go back to it when I might see another opening.

"Okay," I said. "They're going to call you. You'll have to explain that you aren't stalling them. You're trying to get a line through to New York. Arrangements will need to be made through your bank there for the money to be made available to you here. It will take time, but you're working on it and you're not going to let anything go wrong. They are going to get the money."

"Do you think they'll stay on the line long enough for me to tell them all that?"

Just asking the question put a new idea into her head. First she'd only been looking thoughtful, but quickly her look became guarded and suspicious. She was suddenly wary of me.

"Matt," she said. "You're not telling me to keep them on the line so you can tell the police and have the call traced? Don't do that to me, Matt."

"It's what you ought to do, but that will have to be your decision. You don't have to trust me. You'll know I haven't talked to the police. I'm right here with you and I'll be here till the call comes. You can believe me because you'll know that I won't have had any opportunity to tell anyone anything."

None of the suspicion went out of her look.

"You talked Italian to the desk clerk. I don't know what you told him."

"It's been a while since I talked to him. If I'd given him even a hint, you'd have been up to your eyebrows in fuzz by now."

"Forgive me, Matt. I don't know why you put up with me. I don't know why you've ever put up with me."

I was aching to give her a demonstration of my reasons, but it was the wrong time for it.

"When we have him back, I'll show you why."

"You don't really believe it. You don't really believe that we'll ever have him back."

"You're the one who doesn't believe it. I'm going to need a lot more convincing, but let's get back to what you're going to say when that call comes."

"I have all of it. I'll say it."

"Good, and there's more. In Naples you wrote a check for five hundred dollars. What's the most you can write one for?"

"Nothing like they want. I suppose fifty thousand, maybe a hundred thousand."

"You can just walk into a bank here in Palermo and they'll handle that much?"

"I don't know. I've never done it."

We worked at getting it pinned down. She had only the vaguest notion of what her bank balance was, but she had no worry about being overdrawn. The trustees would cover minor sums. They would write scolding letters, but they would cover her. Obviously, that way of doing things wouldn't go for anything like the three million, and obviously she couldn't walk into any Palermo bank and expect them on the spur of the moment to handle a check for any such amount. On one shopping spree or another she had given to couturiers checks for as much as fifty thousand. What it came down to was that the fifty or a hundred thousand she spoke of would be that kind of thing, a check given in payment in an establishment where she was known. The biggest she had ever gone in any European bank had been a thousand. She thought she could go more than that.

"We could cover the town, touring the banks and cashing as much as each one would take on," I suggested. "Your checks, my checks. Between us we could probably piece together twenty to fifty thousand."

"They say three million. They won't look at fifty thousand."

"No, but this is worth trying. You tell them it's going to take time and explain why, and you say that meanwhile just as an indication of your good faith you want to give them everything you can get from the banks here without working through New York. If they'll give you a place where you can deliver this token payment tomorrow noon, you'll have it for them with the balance coming through as soon as it can be set up with the banks."

She brightened. She was ready to grab at anything. She wanted to hang on to some hope.

"You think that will make them more content to wait? It'll keep them from hurting him?"

"It can't do any harm and it just might give me an opening to do something."

"How, Matt? I knew you'd think of something."

"I didn't say it will. It just might."

"It will. It has to. How, Matt? Tell me how."

"They'll give you a place where you're to leave the money. Someone will come and pick it up. If I can follow him, he could lead me to Huddles. That'd be more than half the battle."

She flung her arms around me and kissed me. With the redoubtable Erridge in action she was ready to call it the whole battle. After all, back in Naples I'd done the impossible for her—got her coolie bag back with all its contents intact—and then I hadn't even known her. To her way of thinking, Erridge could do anything.

It was nice having her feel that way. I wished I didn't have to think about the odds and how easily it might be that I would have to disappoint her. I not only didn't want to think about it. I didn't have time for any of that. The call could come through at any moment and she had to be prepared.

"When the phone rings," I told her, "don't grab it. Of course, you'll want to, but don't. Just wait here with your hand on the phone but not lifting it off the cradle. I'll nip into your bedroom and I'll stand in the doorway with the bedroom extension. On my signal you'll lift the phone off the cradle and start talking. That way we can pick them both up simultaneously."

"All right, Matt, but why?"

"Two ears are better than one. Two memories are better

than one. If you answered and then they heard the click of another receiver coming off, they'd get suspicious. We want them to trust you. In the same way, don't hang up your phone until you've seen me hang up."

"We do those together, too, so they won't hear the extra click?"

"We do it after I've heard them hang up and I know we're on a dead line. It'll be all right then if we don't synchronize exactly."

I had no great confidence that any of this would do us any good, but even if it came to nothing, it did have its immediate value. It made her feel that we weren't just sitting there and letting things happen. It gave her the idea that we were on the edge of going into positive action. It could easily prove to be a delusion, but even a delusion would help her through the waiting.

I ordered up some dinner. I wasn't certain that I could get her to eat any of it, but it seemed the best bet to put food in front of her while she was having even this slight lift. If I was ever going to get her to take anything, it would be then. She ate some of it, not much, but some. It would have been more if the telephone hadn't interrupted the meal.

She waited for my signal and she performed perfectly. We were in exact synchronization on the pick up.

"Catherine Martin here," she said.

Her voice sounded great. A little husky with tension but without a tremor.

"Coodlace Marteen?"

It was a man's voice and it was what you might get from an Italian whose English pronunciation was poor to terrible. When I say you might, I mean just that. You might, but it would never be likely. I've never heard an Italian do it exactly that way. It was only a nuance of difference, but it was there. An English-speaker disguising himself behind a vaudeville version of an Italian accent? An Italian trying for a disguise by exaggerating his accent? It could have been either, but either way it wasn't for real.

VII.

He told her that so far Hoodlace was all right. He had come to no harm and he would not be harmed if she followed instructions. He told her to listen carefully because not even a small mistake would be tolerated. If there was even a small slip up, Hoodlace would suffer, and she was to understand that she was talking to a man who knew how to inflict pain and he would do it without hesitation. If the police came anywhere near, the whole deal would be off. She would never again see her brother alive.

She broke in on him to assure him that she was co-operating. She was ready to do anything he said. She would follow his instructions to the letter. There would be no police, not then, not afterward. All she wanted was to have her brother back unharmed.

"That's my part of the bargain," she said, "and I swear I'll keep it, but you must keep your part of the bargain. If you kill him or even just hurt him, you'll be breaking our agreement."

"I am a man of honor, Coodlace."

It was a line out of a bad movie and the delivery was *prosciutto,* raw ham.

He didn't go on with it. He dropped quickly to practical matters. He wanted three million dollars in hundred-dollar bills. He made none of the usual requirements, nothing like unmarked bills, old bills, or bills that would not be in number sequence. He would be calling again, and then he would expect her to tell him that she had the money ready. It would be then that he would give her the payment instructions.

"I'm already working on getting you the money."

She had to break in on him to get even that said. This was no exchange of thoughts or of sentiments. He was just getting her told.

"*Bene*," he said. "*Molto bene*."

His Italian was at least as phony as his English.

"But you have to give me time."

"No time."

"I have to call New York to get the money over here. The bank will need a little time at least to get it together and count it. You'll have it just as soon as I can get it. By tomorrow noon I can . . ."

She went on with it, but she reached him with no more than "tomorrow noon I can." That had been all he'd wanted to hear. He'd hung up on her.

I don't know whether she hadn't heard the click of his ringing off or had gone on talking desperately trying not to believe it. It was hardly possible that she could have been unaware of it when the hotel operator came cutting in on her to tell her that her party was no longer on the line. I hung up the bedroom phone and I took hers out of her hand and hung it up for her.

She tried to hold steady, but it was beyond anything she could handle. She was shaking uncontrollably.

"Matt," she moaned. "He didn't listen. He thinks . . ."

"He thinks he's putting on a tough and terrifying act," I said, breaking in on her and trying to pull her together. "The guy's a clown."

"But he thinks I promised him that I'd have the whole thing for him tomorrow noon and I haven't even got a line through to New York yet. It can take forever and he won't listen."

It didn't take forever. Within the hour her New York line did come through, and all the time we were waiting I worked at damping down her terror. I wished I could believe the stuff I was telling her, but I had to settle for trying to get her to believe it.

"The clown is just putting on an act," I said, "and he doesn't even know how to make it a good act."

I labored the point that he hadn't specified unmarked bills or bills out of number sequence or old bills or bills in the smaller denominations that people take without examining them closely. He'd specified hundreds, and people examine hundreds.

"So he's stupid," she argued. "So after it's all over and he tries to spend the money, he may get caught. What good will that be if he harms Hugh? If he's killed by a fool, Hugh won't be any less dead."

In all the time I'd known her this was the first she'd ever called her brother by anything but the baby-talk nickname. In her mind she was already burying him. You don't carve Huddles on a tombstone.

"He's not going to be dead, Cathy. He's going to be all right. Get straight on your thinking, kid. You've been sure that he's going to be killed because you've been thinking he's in the hands of a kidnapper who knows his job, someone who'll understand the danger of releasing a competent adult who will be able to make identifications. Now you know that it isn't that kind of a kidnapper. This cat thinks he can just take the money and disappear. He doesn't know the first thing about his risks or anything else. He isn't thinking ahead. The kidnapper who kills will be a guy who thinks ahead."

Good reasoning, Charlie?

No. It was only the best I could come up with for pulling her out of her shakes. I was ignoring too many of the surrounding circumstances, and I knew I was doing it.

This bastard was not without funds. To some extent at least Huddles had been financing his own kidnapping. Even though Cathy had already made the shift to giving him the dignity of the dead, in my mind he still was and probably always would be Huddles. It was a silly kid's name for a silly fool who had never grown up anywhere but in his balls.

But enough of that. We're talking money. There had been the Naples partying and the Agrigento partying. I could be sure of those. There may also have been some partying that night in Siracusa or that may have been no more than the delivery of the message. I couldn't know, but it was obvious that all along Huddles had been picking up the checks. It was a cinch that he had been doing more than that. He had been letting himself be milked, and any cash he'd had on him when he was snatched would now also be part of the kidnapper's funds.

There was, furthermore, the gold, all that jewelry that had been stripped off the dying woman on that dark road in Agrigento. Even at fencing rates there had been enough gold there to afford ample provision for running expenses. See how it all adds up?

He collects the ransom. Even in hundreds, three million bucks is thirty thousand bills. Ever seen thirty thousand bills in any denomination all in one place? That's no roll you can tuck down into the pocket of your jeans. It's more like the dimensions of a bale and it's going to weigh. Huddles himself wouldn't weigh any more.

Smaller bills would have to mean even greater bulk and greater weight. So the hundreds are a convenience but only if they can be negotiated without bringing the fuzz down on him and quick. If he would have to use even one of those hundreds right away and right there in Sicily, he would be taking a dangerous risk. What had me bugged was knowing that he didn't have to take any such risk.

He could collect the ransom and, without dipping into it, he could finance getting himself and it out of Sicily. It's a short trip and a cheap one over to North Africa. Algiers? Tangiers? Those are the places where bread is bread and no questions are ever asked.

With what I was telling Cathy, however, I did have a problem. Here I was trying to convince her that the kidnapper was a clown who had gone waltzing into the big time without knowing even the most obvious tricks of the trade.

That might have been all right, but just as I got her sold, she came up with the question that forced me to reverse myself. It called for quick and tricky foot work and I never did quite get it made.

"I see what you mean," she said. "And, of course, you're right. He doesn't know the first thing about money."

"You can figure that he's never had a bill big enough for anyone to look at it twice. He's just a nickles-and-dimes operator playing out of his league. In the end that kind always gets taken."

She shuddered.

"In the end, Matt," she said, "isn't going to be nearly soon enough. If he knew more about money, he would know that he was going to have to wait. He doesn't know that. You're right about him. He's probably never been able to lay his hands on more money than he carried around in his pants pocket. When he has to pay anything out, he just reaches into his pants for it. It takes no time."

"He never reached into his pants for any three million," I said.

"That's just what I'm thinking. He's never done it, so he doesn't know."

"I never have," I argued, "and I do know. It doesn't necessarily follow."

"It follows," she insisted. "He's seen Hugh reach into his pocket and come up with what may be more money than this man ever saw before. It would never occur to him that there could be any limit to what we carry around on us, and if we aren't carrying it around, we just go into a bank and cash a check. He almost certainly saw Hugh do just that and for amounts that looked big to him. If that much, why not three million just like that?"

"Because it's one helluva long way from hundreds or even thousands to that three-million level. I saw you that morning in the bank in Naples, and you were handling five hundred as though it was just old gum wrappers. It didn't make me think there could be no limit for you."

"It's no comparison, Matt. You've never been stupid and you've had experience in handling money, big sums of money too."

"Three million, kid? You've got to be kidding."

I first took to this girl entirely on the way she looked. I had her tagged for all lovely body and no kind of a brain at all. When later I came to dig that she was no fool and that it was only that she had never in her life had to be wise about money, it got to be more than just lusting after her. Hell, I was in love with her. Now I was wishing she had, in fact, been what I had first taken her for, complete idiocy in a gorgeous housing. It would have been a lot easier to channel her thinking in the way I would have liked it to go.

"When you're working," she said, "it's always on something big, things so big that three million won't even get them started. I don't know exactly what bridges and dams and stuff like that might cost, but I know it has to be hundreds of millions when it isn't billions."

"Not always and it's never my money."

"Even if it's only sometimes, even if it's only been once, even if you didn't handle any of it, you were there and you saw those sums go by. You know how money works and you know how banks work."

"Not for coming up with anything like three million in cash," I said. "Money like that, when it moves legally, never moves in the form of cash. It's just a ledger entry that comes off one set of books and goes onto another. I have seen checks for three million and more. They've even passed through my hands, but never in cash."

That was only a half truth or you can fraction it smaller than a half. I had handled cash payrolls that ran into the upper brackets. For purposes of argument I was choosing to forget that detail. She didn't catch me out on it because there was no way for her to know. She had never met a payroll and she had never picked up a pay envelope.

She hit me at a subtler level.

"Just knowing it's always done by check," she insisted, "tells you that it wouldn't be easy to do it in cash, that it would take time."

"I never thought of it that way until I had to today," I said. "I just thought that checks were safer. Until I found myself trying to visualize the weight and the bulk of thirty thousand hundred-dollar bills, I never even had the thought that a check is lighter to lift. You don't need as much muscle for carrying it around. You don't have to know or to have experience. The minute you're confronted with the thought, it becomes obvious. It has to be obvious to anyone, even this silly clown."

"Matt," she groaned. "It isn't. You know it isn't. It's not

at all obvious to him, and he wouldn't wait to listen. He never gave me a chance to put the idea into his head. I can't possibly have the money for him by tomorrow noon, and he's going to do something horrible to Hugh."

"Nonsense. That was just talk. He put that in only to frighten you. Don't forget this is bargaining country, and in bargaining you come on strong. You leave plenty of leeway for getting yourself whittled down. He says no delay. He makes any threat he thinks will scare you the most."

"Thinks, Matt? He has scared me. I've never been so scared."

"Of course, you are. It's the way he wants you to be. It's the way he's going to try to keep you. He wants you to be so frightened of the necessary delay that you'll push your hardest to speed things up. He wants you so scared that the first moment you have the money in hand, you'll run to hand it to him."

I was doing my best, and I wasn't doing too well. It was a relief to have it interrupted by the New York call.

In placing the call she had asked for a man whose name I'm going to hold back. You don't need it. You can take my word for it. It was one of those names that mean money and power anywhere in the world.

"Uncle Jimmie," she began.

"Catherine," Uncle Jimmie barked. "Are you in Palermo?"

(A kid is caught with his hand in the cookie jar. "Junior, are you eating between meals?" It was that approach.)

"I'm calling from Palermo," she said, and she tried to get on with it.

Uncle Jimmie wasn't ready to listen to anything.

"I'd like you to get out of there at once. It's no place for you to be. I suppose you are with Hugh, but neither of you should be in a place like that. Capri, Cannes, Sardinia,

Portofino, the Lido. You have a world of suitable places to
go to and you go to Palermo. Let me talk to Hugh."

"You can't talk to Hugh, he's . . ."

He didn't let her finish what she was about to say. I wondered whether he ever let anyone finish what they had to
say. Uncle Jimmie was a teller, and I don't mean the kind
they have in banks. He wasn't anybody's listener. I was
hearing all this because we were following the same routine
with the two phones on all calls.

When the operator had said she had the New York line,
I'd started to hang up. Nobody had given me a license for
eavesdropping on all her phone calls, but she shook her
head at me and asked me to stay on. She wanted me to
hear.

Uncle Jimmie was horrified.

"Hugh isn't with you?" he howled. "You're in Palermo
alone?"

"He's here but he can't come to the phone. He'll call you
as soon as he can, and we'll go any place you want us to go
just as soon as we can. That's a promise, Uncle Jimmie, but
first I have to have three million dollars just as fast as you
can get it to me. Please, Uncle Jimmie. How quickly can I
have it?"

She got no direct answer. She got a discussion instead.
Now Uncle Jimmie was all strained patience and un-
strained asperity. She didn't attempt to cut him short. I
could guess that she had learned that the quickest way to
get through to him would be by way of sitting through the
full lecture and taking it in silence.

"Catherine," he said. "I was looking at your accounts
only this morning. Hugh has been drawing at about his cus-
tomary mad rate, but I was beginning to be a little en-
couraged about you. Judging from your recent with-

drawals, I was beginning to hope that you might be starting to be more sensible."

He was wrong about that, of course, and I could hardly claim that under my good influence she was a changed girl. It was just that, compared with all their usual playgrounds —those places he had just given his stamp of approval— Naples and Sicily, if they weren't poor men's paradises, did at least offer fewer opportunities for big spending.

"But now you've gone completely mad," he continued. "I know that neither Hugh nor you has any head for figures. I know you blithely ignore anything as boring as keeping your checkbooks balanced, but even you, my child, cannot possibly be thinking that, just because for a short time your withdrawals have been noticeably more modest, you could have built up a balance of anything even approaching three million dollars."

"I know I haven't. That's why I'm calling you. I know you'll have to advance it. How . . ."

I knew she was about to ask him how soon she could have it. Uncle Jimmie may have known it as well. He wasn't waiting for her to get any more of the question out.

"How, indeed," he exploded. "You may very well ask how, my child. The answer is no possible way. Put it out of your mind. Forget it. Even for you it's too absurd."

"But it's a matter of life and death."

"Catherine, my dear. I wish you wouldn't overdramatize yourself. It's vulgar."

"Uncle Jimmie, you must listen to me. I'm not overdramatizing. I'm being calm. I don't know how I can be so calm, but I'm controlling myself. Believe me."

"Child, you don't sound calm. You're hysterical."

"You don't know. I should be screaming. I should be crying."

"Don't. The trans-Atlantic telephone is not for screaming

and crying. You want three million dollars. What do you want it for?"

"It isn't that I just want it. I must have it. I have no choice."

"You know that isn't an answer. You are asking me to invade principle for three million dollars without even knowing what you intend to do with it. Do you have any idea of what three million dollars is? I don't think you do. If you did, you wouldn't dream of making such a demand."

"I'm not making the demand."

"Then what are you doing?"

"I'm telling you that I have to have it because it is a question of life or death."

"Catherine, if you persist in using that ridiculous, hysterical phrase, we won't be able to discuss this."

"Why do you want us out of Palermo?"

I would have liked to drop the phone and kiss her. This was Matt's clever girl. She was trying to avoid saying what she couldn't safely say over the telephone, and she was finding a way of getting the idea across without saying the words.

"I should think it would be obvious," Uncle Jimmie huffed. "Sicily is dangerous. It's home base for the Mafia. The whole island is overrun with gangsters and bandits. Murder is a commonplace there. One or both of you could be kidnapped and held for ransom. It's not as though people wouldn't know who you are. Those Mafia bandits make a point of knowing. Don't think they'll mistake you for some schoolteacher who is traveling on a budget. They can kidnap you and ask me for any amount of money."

She could have told him that he was the one who was talking hysterical nonsense. Any fool should know that, with the whole world on wings, there aren't any places any more that are particularly dangerous or any places that are specially safe.

Of course, she didn't. She wasn't on the phone for Uncle Jimmie's enlightenment. He had come to the edge of understanding. She had to be in there to give him the extra little push he needed.

"Any amount of money," she said. "Any amount like three million."

There were some moments of silence after that. It wasn't total silence. There was a sound that you could have thought might be a wind coming up over the Atlantic, but you can't hear anything like that over the trans-Atlantic telephone. It was Uncle Jimmie sucking in his breath.

When he spoke again, he was in a much different tone. He was no longer thundering, no longer pontificating.

"Can you tell me where you are?" he asked.

She gave him the name of the hotel.

"Free to come and go?"

"Except that I must stay by the telephone. There could be a call anytime."

"From Hugh or about him?"

"Yes."

"Have you called the police?"

"No."

"That's the first thing you must do."

"It's the last thing I can do."

"Oh, come, child."

"Uncle Jimmie, you must understand. It's a matter of life and death."

"All right, all right. Have you talked to the American consul?"

"No. I can't risk talking to anyone."

He didn't push it. He'd heard enough. Now he was all business, all efficiency.

"How soon do you need the money?"

"Tomorrow noon. Three million in hundred-dollar bills."

"Tomorrow noon. You'll have to have a postponement."

"I tried to explain that it would probably be impossible to do it that quickly, but he wouldn't listen. He hung up before I could even begin to explain."

"No way you can reach them?"

"He calls me. I have to stay by the phone."

"Yes. Naturally it would be that way. All right, Catherine. Be a good girl. Be calm. Don't worry. We have the advantage of the time difference. It's only four o'clock here in New York. That gives me at least three hours before I'll have to be flying to Rome. It's a tight schedule, but I can arrange for the money in that time."

"Can you reach the others that fast, or can you do that much money without them?"

The others, I could guess, would be other administrators of the Martin trusts.

"Leave it to me, child. With them or without them I'll do it. I'll be landing in Rome by midmorning. I won't depend on any scheduled connection to Palermo. I can have a charter waiting for me at Leonardo da Vinci. I'll be with you by noon. I promise. You'll leave the negotiations to me."

"You're not going to bargain with them?"

"I'll do only what is best for Hugh. Hundred-dollar bills. Old bills? Unmarked? Not in series?"

"So far he hasn't said anything about any of that. Just three million dollars, and it has to be all in hundred-dollar bills."

"All right, my dear. We'd better ring off now and let me get at it. I shall see you tomorrow."

"Uncle Jimmie."

"Yes, my dear. What is it?"

"I'm sorry we're such a worry to you."

"No time for that now."

"I love you, Uncle Jimmie."

He didn't tell her there was no time for that. Even though there are probably not many people who'll ever believe it, the man wasn't a computer in pants. He was a man. He was that much human.

"You handled that well," I told her when we'd hung up.

I wasn't about to tell her that it had been better managed than she had intended it to be. Although she had carefully skirted any use of the words, kidnapping or ransom, she had been forced to come close to them before she could make Uncle Jimmie understand.

I couldn't believe that, even without coming that close, she wouldn't have made a hotel switchboard operator understand. In some ordinary Italian hotel it might have been that the operator's English would not have been up to the job of penetrating the screen of caution Cathy had put around her words. This, however, was no ordinary Italian hotel. It was a Cuddles-and-Huddles-type hotel, Palermo's bid for the international-jet-set, grande-luxe trade. European hotels at that level are manned by effectively polylingual staffs.

Switchboard operators, of course, do not listen to every call that passes through the switchboard. There could have been no certainty that the operator listened in on the call from the kidnapper. When, however, an urgent call goes through for a man whose name is a world-wide synonym for money, you're going to be hard put to find the operator who will not listen in.

So I was just about certain that they had been overheard and understood. I was hardly less certain that the operator would not just sit on the information. The news was going to get to the fuzz if it had not already been conveyed to them.

That was going to be a bad moment when the officers of the law turned up. Cathy was going to go into a fresh panic, but I could see no way that it wouldn't be all to the good. I knew that it could be that police participation mightn't help, but I was convinced that it couldn't hurt.

Don't think that I didn't recognize the possibility that the kidnapper might kill Hugh Martin. I did recognize it. In fact, I was thinking that it was a great likelihood. I believed the threat, but I didn't believe that it hung on anything Cathy might or might not do. It was because I was convinced that paying the ransom and doing everything exactly as the kidnapper said it was to be done was not going to be enough to save Huddles that I was so ready to welcome police intervention. We could be ending up with Huddles dead, but it would not be because the police came into it. It would be because the kidnapper had never intended to let him go on living.

For these reasons it was with a mixture of apprehension and hope that I was waiting for the fuzz to turn up. What came, however, was something I never expected.

It was a small package addressed to Cathy and even at first glance we knew who sent it. The address was done as it had been on the envelope of the ransom note: her name clipped out of a magazine and pasted to the wrapping paper.

I opened it for her. Her hands were shaking so much that she couldn't get her fingers on the string. Inside the paper was a candy box but not a chance that anybody was sending her chocolates. Pasted to the box in assembled single printed words there was another message.

"Get moving while he still has the other one."

I turned to block her view of the box. I didn't know that

I could bring it off to stop her looking at what was in the box, but I had to make the try.

It was no good. She flared up in resentment at my trying to shield her. Her anger steadied her hands. She reached around and grabbed the box from me. It would have been no good fighting her for it. Whatever she was going to find inside it, she would find. I could grab it back from her and go off somewhere to open it but it would only be the difference between her seeing what was in it or imagining the worst.

She lifted the lid. Inside there was an oilskin tobacco pouch. She unrolled it and its contents fell out. It was an ear, a human ear with the blood dried on it. She stood for a moment or two, looking down at it while belief was taking hold.

When she swayed, I caught her and she collapsed in my arms. I carried her into the bedroom and laid her on the bed. She was out cold. I remembered a bottle of Armagnac in my room. Leaving her on the bed, I ran out of the suite and down the hall to my room. Just bringing her out of the faint, I was thinking, wasn't going to be enough. I wanted to bring her out with a slug of the brandy husky enough so it could substitute for the passed-out-with-shock situation a preferable passed-out-drunk.

If I was gone from her suite as much as two minutes, that was a lot. I just galloped down the hall, unlocked the door to my room, grabbed the Armagnac bottle off the table, and ran back with it.

The door to the suite was standing open. I hadn't left it that way. I clearly remembered slamming it shut after me just as, on leaving my room with the Armagnac, I had slammed that door shut behind me. In neither case had I stopped to lock the door. I wasn't taking the time for anything like that. If I was remembering the Boy Scout manual correctly, in an emergency you acted and acted fast. You wasted no time worrying about security.

Running down toward her rooms, I noticed that a swinging door was swinging just beyond her suite. That door led to the outer hall and the elevators. For the moment I ignored it. I was totally focused on bringing the Armagnac and Cathy together and as quickly as possible.

In her sitting room, however, I was brought up short. On the table where she had unwrapped the ear there sat all the wrappings, the paper, the string, the candy box, the tobacco pouch. Only the ear was gone. Through the open door to the bedroom I could see her where I'd stretched her out on the bed. She was still passed out. I had been that quick. She was young and she was healthy, and for the young and healthy consciousness comes back pretty fast. I didn't wait for it. Leaving the Armagnac bottle on the table, I headed for that swinging door I had seen on the swing.

VIII.

Call it luck or call it another lovable aspect of the Italian scene. Elevator service in that great country is nowhere fast and nowhere frequent, not even in business-always-as-usual, super-efficient Milan. This, furthermore, was not Milan. It was Sicily, the ultimate in *dolce-far-niente* country. If the elevator operators find it sweet to do nothing, they have the co-operation of beautifully sluggish elevator mechanisms. Even in this most de luxe of de luxe establishments the cars rose and fell under the control of *dolce-far-niente* machinery.

In most places somewhere in the vicinity of the elevators and in a location well marked and easy to find, you'll come on the fire stairs. No so here. Here Italian tact intervenes. Italian thinking has it that the suggestion of the possibility of a hotel fire could only depress people, and Italian hotelkeepers are too warm hearted and hospitable to risk depressing a guest. I have no doubt that the hotel did have fire stairs, but they were kept in some remote and unseen place where there was no danger that anyone might find them and be kicked off into a disquieting train of thought.

When I came through the swinging doors to the outer hall, therefore, he was still there waiting for an elevator to come up and take him away. I knew him on sight and it had to be that he knew me. I had, after all, caught little more than a glimpse of him. He had been engaged for the job of keeping an eye on me with a view toward manhandling me if or when it might have become necessary.

It was one of the muscle-heavy curly tops Huddles had in the Rolls with him that first morning back in Naples.

I thought of the man who needed a light when we turned our backs on Huddles in Segesta. I had seen him only from a difficult angle, but even so I had been fairly sure that it was one of that pair I had seen in Naples, not this one but his buddy. Although he did glance back over his shoulder when he heard the door swing behind him, he promptly returned his gaze to the doors to the elevator shafts. He was pretending that I was just another guy waiting for an elevator.

I gave it the same treatment, the one quick glance and after that the big show of no interest. We waited for the elevator together and, when it came, we rode down to the lobby together.

Downstairs he behaved as though he had all the time in the world. He sauntered around the lobby, looking things over. He stationed himself at the newspaper stand and looked at magazines. He didn't look like a man who would be much given to reading or even like one who would know how to read, but he, nevertheless, managed to look natural enough. He concentrated on the right magazines. Any man, after all, can read tits.

So I was also a man with time on his hands. I wandered the lobby. I looked at postcards.

Suddenly he made a dash for the door. You know, a guy is just loafing along when suddenly it comes to him that he has an important date he's been letting slip his mind. I hit the door right at his heels. If he had been any good at this game, he would have known, but he wasn't much good at it. I can only suppose that the act I'd been putting on had been good enough.

Once in the open, he headed straight for a car parked out front. Baby was out there, too. I'd had her brought out of the hotel garage when I'd planned to have her take us to dinner. When the ransom message changed our routine for the evening, I had used her in that futile pursuit of the first messenger. When we came back from that, I'd had other things on my mind and hadn't thought of having her returned to the garage.

Among the cars sitting out there the one he was headed for was the standout. It was the tiniest and tinniest of all economy mini-jobs. It had seen better days and it had met in violent contact better cars. No more than the absolutely necessary had ever been done to it to keep it on the road. It bore its full collection of scars and they were so numerous that even its dents had dents.

I got a good look at it and at its license plate. It had a Sicilian registration that indicated that its home port would be somewhere in the middle of the island, in an area that is sliced through by the Palermo-Catania *autostrada*. Italian license plates have letters and numbers. The letters indicate the city or the district in which the car is registered.

Even if he hadn't started toward it, I would have known that it had to be his car. There wasn't another thing around there that stood on wheels and that didn't gleam. This one heap alone looked as though it had never known the gentle touch of the chamois. This one alone was not a custom-made job.

I could say that it went with the way he himself looked, but you can't know much these days from the way people look. There was a time when the patched blue jeans and fisherman's striped jersey and the beat-up sandals would have earned him nothing but a quick heave-ho from the hotel doorman. Nowadays it gets a cat a full measure of bowing and scraping because the wearer might well be the hotel's most valued patron and its most lavish tipper.

After all, how is a hotel doorman to know which pair of jeans won its patches in the ordinary, old-fashioned way and which had them applied in the atelier of some Paris or Rome couturier where the exact placement of every stitch might determine the fashion trends for a generation?

He was halfway across to the car when he finally became aware that he had me on his tail. Suddenly that appointment he'd remembered wasn't so important after all. It could wait, and since he was there at that hotel, it would have been a shame not to take a night-time stroll through its famous gardens. Granted that night is no time for seeing gardens, he could nevertheless stroll about in it and smell it.

He turned away from the car and wandered off into the shrubbery. I wandered after him. I was thinking that he couldn't have chosen a better spot for my purposes. In there among the shrubs I was going to catch up with him and I was going to work him over. Before I was through with him I was planning to have him singing like a nightingale. If I didn't succeed, it was going to be only because he had no voice. I was certain he did have a voice.

He dove into the shrubbery and I dove after him. I suppose I was unduly hooked on the idea that he wanted nothing but to avoid me. I had myself so built up on what I was going to do to him that I fell into the trap of thinking that he would also know what I had in store for him and would be bent only on escaping me.

I don't know that it made any difference. I had no choice but to keep on him until I could have him alone and in a place where I could have at him undisturbed.

I dove into the shrubbery, and in mid-dive I made anesthetizing contact with a set of brass knuckles.

Since this is the nature of such blows, at the time I hadn't the first idea of what hit me. It's like that. You're there and then you're not there, and after a while you come back and you start trying to reconstruct. If you have been around enough and in your time you have given and taken your quota of smacks in the jaw, from an inspection of the size and nature of your contusions and abrasions you can do a lot of reconstructing, like knowing a brass-knuck job from a bare-knuck job.

I heaved to my feet and groped my way clear of the bushes. I looked just in case, but I saw no more than I had expected to see. Tiny Tin was gone and nobody had to tell me that my man was gone with it. Although immediate pursuit was indicated, it didn't need to be so immediate that I couldn't stop to do a little something for Cathy.

Since any present possibility of keeping him in sight had gone glimmering, I was going to have to let everything ride on the chance that I would be able to pick him up again. Whether or not I was going to manage to bring that off was going to hinge on several things, but none of them was going to be making every second count. At that moment, although speed was not to be disdained, it was not of the essence.

The one obstacle was my jaw. From the way it felt in itself and from the way it felt under the touch of my fingertips, I knew that I couldn't hope that it would be unnoticeable. Going back through the lobby and up in the elevator with my too obviously battered chin hanging out didn't worry me. That I could carry off by putting on one of those but-you-ought-to-see-the-other-guy looks.

I didn't want to fall into any spot where I would have to go into conversation about it. That could take more time than I had. Also with the strong possibility that the fuzz was on the way, talk could delay me long enough to hold me in the hotel until after their arrival and then I might not be able to break loose at all, at least not without telling them where I was going.

I know, Charlie, I know. I had been all for bringing them in and I still wanted them in, but it had to be with them working on their own. It seemed to me that what I had to do would be a one-man job, and I was the one man.

So instead of barging over to the desk and telling the desk clerk what he had to know and what I wanted him to do, I sailed straight through to the elevators and went back upstairs. It was the best way to do it, particularly since I had to go up there anyhow. There was something I needed from my room.

I was aching to go back to Cathy, if only to see how she was, but I put myself on a short leash and made myself come to heel. I went to my room, picked up the phone and asked for the desk. I told the clerk that I wanted him to locate an English-speaking doctor. I demanded a good one and one that could be produced in nothing flat. He was to go to Miss Martin's suite. He was going to find her in a clearly nervous state, probably in need of sedation. He was to do whatever he could for her, and I would like it if he installed a team of English-speaking nurses to be with her around the clock.

If Miss Martin inquired for me, he was to tell her that I'd had to go out on her business and that things were looking up.

While I was shooting him all this stuff, I was carrying the phone wedged between my ear and my shoulder so I could dig in my luggage for what I needed. I had no trouble finding the things. I've spent too many years wandering the world not to know how to pack. That's one of the Erridge talents, packing.

"Should the doctor see you before you go?" the clerk asked.

"I can't wait for him. I haven't the time and there isn't anything I could tell him that he won't find out for himself as soon as he's seen Miss Martin."

"Yes, Mr. Erridge, but I was thinking for you."

My passage through the lobby hadn't gone unobserved.

"Nothing wrong with me that won't heal itself," I said, and I hung up.

With a telephone you can do things that are not as easy face to face.

I had found everything and now there was nothing left to do but stow it about my person where it would be most handy. I loaded the revolver and tucked it in my belt. A supply of extra shells I dropped into my coat pocket.

That was it. I was ready. Going back out to the elevators I wouldn't let myself even look in the direction of Cathy's door. It's only so far that even a man of steel can go in the way of resisting temptation and, whenever I got to thinking about Cathy, I felt more like a man of butter. It could even be butter on a hot day.

I mounted the Porsche and took off. Before I was clear of the hotel grounds a roaring procession passed me going the other way. The fuzz was coming in for its landing. I had made the right guess on the switchboard operator. I couldn't feel too good about poor Cathy left to take on all those *carabinieri* alone, but there was no help for that, and I had to be glad I was running clear before they could know they wanted me.

That I had made a good guess on the switchboard operator I found encouraging. I had everything riding on my other guesses proving to be equally sound. Having this evidence that the Erridge guessing gauges were in solid working order handed me a much needed lift.

To get from the hotel to the Palermo-Catania *autostrada* you have to work your way through the city traffic from one end of Palermo to the other. You have a wide choice of streets to do it on. The chance that I might choose the same route as Tiny Tin had taken was more than remote and, even if such a miracle did come my way, there was next to no possibility that I could catch up with him before he cleared Palermo. Obviously, Baby had more speed in her than Tiny Tin could ever aspire to, but, riding from traffic light to traffic light in streets that were choked with cars, her speed could never come into play.

It didn't matter. Everything was hanging on my hunch that he would be taking the *autostrada* and, if that hunch was to do me any good, he was going to have to be on it before me. Once on that high-speed highway, I could let Baby have her head, and I hadn't the first doubt that I could overtake Tiny Tin well before it could cover the hundred kilometers and more that lie between Palermo and the home-base territory indicated by its license plate. Making the good speed that could put me on the *autostrada* ahead of brass knucks would do nothing but screw me up. I had to follow him to where he was going. I couldn't lead him. He knew where it was and I didn't.

As I'd expected, it took me a good half hour to make it through the city, but then we were out in the open and I got Baby to rolling. As we moved along, I was trying to think ahead. When I had seen this guy and his buddy back in Naples where they had been tailing me with Huddles in the Rolls, I had pegged the two of them as muscular persuaders of the type that always worked in pairs. Now I had to amend that to take into consideration the likelihood that there were other kinds of duty they could pull in which they could operate as soloists.

I was more than average certain that it had been one of them in need of a light at Segesta with every indication that there he had been working as a single. Now it had been the other one at the hotel, and he had also been alone. I'd had a good look at his car and there had been nobody waiting for him in it. At least there had been nobody I could see.

His buddy could have been there crouched down out of sight, but I couldn't see any reason for his doing anything like that. It was even more possible that at Segesta this bimbo had been somewhere about waiting in a car while the other one went back of the shed to hit Huddles for a light. I was figuring that when I caught up with him, there would be only the one of him, but I was telling myself at the same time that it wasn't something I could be counting on.

Anywhere along the way this guy could have picked up a passenger or passengers. I could think of no reason why he should, but then nobody could tell me that I was involved in anything that looked like a reasonable course of events.

Could there be any reason why, immediately after delivering the ear, he would at great risk jump in to snatch it back? Also, why should the ear be delivered so soon, and why should it have been delivered at all? Cathy had promised to comply with every demand. She had tried to suggest that there might be a little necessary delay, but she had been told off on that and then given no opportunity even to discuss the orders she had been given.

I had been comfortably certain that I was understanding what went on, but this ear bit had me reeling. I couldn't get it to read for anything but gratuitous sadism, but even that left too much unexplained. There had to be some reason for the here-it-is-and-here-it-isn't routine. It didn't have to be a good reason, only one that could have seemed good to our curly-topped bully boy, but even at that level I couldn't make it out.

I tried hard to think with his mind, but his performance had been so idiotic that the more I thought about it the more I came around to wondering whether it wasn't possible that he just didn't have a mind.

After about an hour of highway driving my lights picked him up. I pulled up only close enough to read the license plate so I could be certain I did have the right car. This would hardly be a unique heap, but the plate number cinched it for me. Once I was satisfied, I dropped back until I had Baby positioned at a distance at which I could just keep his taillights in sight. Holding her to his speed, I followed along that way.

I had no way of knowing whether he was aware that I was sitting on his tail. He had to know that a car had come up behind him and then dropped back, but he couldn't have known what car. I had come up on him with my high beams on.

Once I had dropped back, there was nothing for him to see, nothing but my pair of headlights. He could know that there was a car hanging on at a distance behind him, he had to be wondering whether he was being followed.

All this, of course, was predicated on the assumption that he was something less than totally witless, and I was asking myself whether I could make any such assumption about a man who delivered the ear and then promptly snatched it away.

I rode his tail for the better part of a second hour and what had been inexplicable before began to look even worse. I was thinking about the elapsed time between the phone call and the delivery of the ear. There hadn't been enough of it for any round trip between the Palermo hotel and wherever it would now be that I was being led.

It would need to have been that the whole thing had been set up on a predetermined schedule without any waiting for Cathy's response, a set time for the delivery of the ransom note and a set time for the delivery of the ear with the phone call inserted neatly between. If on my earlier thinking I couldn't understand the savagery of the severed ear coming so much too early in the game, it had now come to look as though it had been even earlier than I thought.

There was only one other possibility and that would be that my man was smarter than he looked. It could have been that he wasn't leading me to the kidnap hideaway at all, that with every mile I followed him I was being drawn farther off the trail.

It was something to worry about, but then suddenly his taillights were gone and that was something more immediate to worry about.

A sudden dip in the road could have taken them away from me momentarily, but it wasn't that I lost them only for a moment. They were gone and they stayed gone. Also, I was remembering that this was the *autostrada,* a beautifully engineered highway that has no sudden dips in it. It did its ups and downs in smoothly modulated grades and it turned its corners in broad sweeps.

It couldn't be that he had turned off and left the *autostrada.* Its exit ramps are as well designed as the rest of it, and they take you out in broad, gradual turns. If he had taken that kind of a turnoff, his lights wouldn't have done this sort of sudden disappearance. I would instead have seen them seem to draw together as the turn swung them toward me giving me a profile view. It could have been only after that they would have disappeared.

I had to read it for a discouraging indication that he

wasn't quite as brainless as I had been letting myself think. Since I persisted in following his lights, he was going to take care of that by leaving me with no lights to follow. He could ride the *autostrada* dark. Dangerous? Yes, but only within limits. The *autostrada* is built in one-way lanes, so there was no need to worry about any oncoming cars. Without lights, however, there was a chance that he could miss a curve and go off the road; but assuming that he had driven this stretch often, I could guess that he knew it well enough to drive it by the seat of his pants.

The danger, therefore, boiled down to only two unavoidable hazards. A faster car roaring up behind him might not see him soon enough to avoid a rear-end collision. Some other car riding ahead of him without lights he would never see at all. He wouldn't even know it was there until he found out by smashing into its rear.

Whatever else it might mean, it unquestionably did mean one thing. He was doing some thinking. Once I'd tumbled to that, I was back at the old game, trying to think with his mind. Flaky as the guy seemed to be, he could hardly have been planning to do much of the *autostrada* without lights. He wasn't riding some back-country track through the other side of nowhere. He was on a road that was heavily patrolled all day and all night.

Much as he might be wanting to lose me, he could hardly be in the market for finding the fuzz. Reading my odometer and drawing myself a mental map, I worked at building myself a picture of what he was doing. The point at which I'd lost his lights had been about a kilometer or two short of a turnoff. After that one there was not going to be another for something like eighty kilometers. All that way with no lights was too stupid for even this guy who had played his crazy game with the ear.

The risk of one or two kilometers, however, he would

take, and it hadn't been even that much. I was remembering to deduct the lead space I had been allowing him. He
was taking the turnoff, and he had fixed it so I couldn't see
him go.

I wanted to think that it had to mean that he was coming
close to the kidnap hideaway, close enough so that he had
to start working at losing me. There was the other possibility, however, and I didn't want to think about that one.
If he had been leading me off the trail, he could have
reached the place where he thought he'd drawn me far
enough away and he could now afford to lose me. I kept
my mind on Tiny Tin's registration. It was my one comfort.
We were in the right area for that license plate.

I stepped up my speed. I was all right as far as the
turnoff from the *autostrada,* and after that I would be all
right on the little mountain road, but only until he reached
the place where the first branch track might take him off it.
Before that I had to catch up with him. If I didn't, I would
have lost him.

I knew the *autostrada,* but he would be taking a back
road. Once we'd be on that, I was not going to be able to
anticipate anything and there was no map to help me. If I
didn't know this particular road, I had, one time or another, been over too many like it. Taking off from it there
would be many mountain tracks that didn't even show on
any map. He would have to be taking one of those. Kidnap
hideaways don't grow right out on anybody's road. I was
clinging to that. He had to be heading for the hideaway
even though the timing was so wrong.

Once I was off the *autostrada,* everything was going to
depend on Baby catching up with Tiny Tin before we
would come to the first of those mountain trails and on sitting so close on his tail that even on the tightest of hairpin
curves he couldn't for a moment be out of my sight.

To expect that with me following him that close he was just going to roll on and lead me anywhere would certainly be to hope for too much. Somewhere short of that he was going to have to stand and fight, and that would be where Erridge was going to need to take over. I was going to have to hold him and make him talk.

Ordinarily, sadism is not my bag, but even in gentler characters than I've ever pretended to be there can come those times when some buried strain of it will surface and take over. I must admit that I'd begun to look forward to it. Maybe it was because I'd begun to take too much pleasure in the thought that my better sense stepped in and slapped me down.

What was to say that he would have to stand and fight? Mightn't he have another alternative? Like what? Like letting Baby hold his tail all the way into the hideaway. There he wouldn't be facing me alone. He'd have buddies available to back his hand. They were holding one prisoner. If forced into it, would they be averse to holding two?

I couldn't let it bug me. Nobody had given me any guarantees that this was going to be easy. There was nothing for it but to ride with it and play it as it came. If I could have believed that this lug I was trailing could be any kind of a brain, I could have held the thought that he was going to stand and fight. How could he not consider the possibility that I was no lone operator, that instead I was something like a decoy for the fuzz and that any place I was led they would follow?

It was a nice idea but I had too good a notion of just how it could be that he could not consider it. I'd had too little indication that inside that curly head of his he was carrying anything equipped for the consideration of even the most obvious possibilities.

Leaving the *autostrada,* I had to cut down on Baby's

speed. Right from its start that side road was climbing steeply. It went into a quick succession of switchbacks and the curves were not banked in any way that could make it easier for your wheels to hold the road. Off the *autostrada* my speed advantage was down the drain.

On that poorly engineered mountain track I couldn't draw on it enough to make much difference. It would have been impossible even if the surface had been in any sort of decent condition, but that it wasn't. It was rutted and potholed, but the ruts and the potholes were the least of it. I was hitting places where the road was all but washed away, barely enough of it left for sneaking Baby through.

One thing was sure. Tiny Tin couldn't be taking this one without its lights. Of course, Baby couldn't do it either. I would be spotting him long before I would catch up with him and he would be spotting me just as soon. It would be great if, on spotting him, I could close in on him fast, but on this road there was going to be no chance.

There was no doubt that I would be able to close in on him, however gradually. There would be a gain on every turn, and that road was nothing but turns all the way. Baby handles. She handles like a dream, and I was playing her great maneuverability for all it was worth. We also had another thing riding with us, Baby and I, and that was the big one. Going upgrade, Tiny Tin huffed and puffed and labored foot by foot. Baby has the climb of a mountain goat except that hers is a lot smoother.

I can't pretend that luck wasn't riding with me. That road might have been built exactly to specifications so that it could serve Erridge's need. It climbed and climbed and nothing wider than a footpath took off from it. I did recognize that, since he seemed to be carrying no more freight than the one ear, he could switch to going it on foot, but he could hardly do that without letting me know it. I would come on Tiny Tin where he would have abandoned it. There was no place where he could get a car off the road and conceal it. At least up to that point in the climb I had come on no such place.

It was after only about a quarter of an hour of climbing that I picked up the twin red of a pair of taillights. It had to be my man. There had been no car between us on the *autostrada* and, since leaving the *autostrada*, there had been no road junction. Obviously then, there had been no place where another heap could have come in.

If I had been pushing Baby to every last thing she could do on a road like that, I now worked at finding all the little extras I could get out of her. Bit by bit we closed in on Tiny Tin, and in less than five minutes we were within inches of handing him an automotive goose. I could see the guy hunched over the wheel. I could sense his desperate urge to look back over his shoulder at me, but it was obvious that he didn't dare risk it. He had to give everything he had to holding Tiny Tin on the road.

He kept going, and I held in just as tight behind him as I could be without touching. We rode along that way for all of an hour, but in all that time we made only a little more than thirty kilometers. That's about twenty miles which should give you some idea of how we were slowed down to Tiny Tin's crawl.

The hands on my dashboard clock had climbed to midnight and were beginning the slide down toward one. I got to thinking that following him as close as I was and keeping the pressure steadily on him, I was beginning to smell his sweat. It's a good bet that I did have him sweating, but it's an even better bet that what I was smelling was my own.

We came to the first turnoff and he passed it by. Within a quarter of a mile after it we came to a second one. That one he took. I wondered, as I followed him into it, how far he could take it. At its beginning it seemed to be only barely passable and it gave every promise of getting worse as it went along.

He didn't stay with it for any distance. About a hundred yards in he pulled to a stop. I stopped right behind him, pulled my gun, and vaulted out of the Porsche. He was sitting tight in Tiny Tin. I had been worried for fear that he might do a quick dismount and take off into the brush where I might easily lose him. I had moved fast in an effort to forestall that but the way he was sitting when I came up to him, I could see I had forestalled nothing. He had never had any plans.

He looked at the gun in my hand but he didn't dwell on it. He stayed with it only long enough to recognize it for what it was and then, in fine disregard of it, he shifted his gaze to meet me eye to eye. It wasn't a stare-down or anything like that. He was just not afraid and not ashamed. He had no trouble looking me in the eye.

"I was wrong not to kill you when I could," he said. "I don't know why I didn't want to."

"What are you looking for then?" I asked, "Gratitude? Waiting for me to say thank you?"

I said it.

"Grazie."

Remember this was Brainless. He came back at me and rocked me on my heels.

"Prego," he said.

From this lug, Charlie? Humor yet? Irony? Playing along with his welcome to my thank you.

If that didn't take care of the amenities, I could think of nothing else that might have been required.

"You know what I want," I said.

"You can't have it. I won't give it to you. You'll have to kill me first."

"I'm not going to kill you. I'm just going to cripple you. A bullet in your leg. If that doesn't do it, a bullet in your other leg. Then if I have to, in one arm, in the other arm, here and there. I've a good supply of ammunition, but all the same I'll run out of bullets before I run out of places where I can shoot you without killing you."

"I don't care what you do, I'm not giving it to you."

His words came in gasps. The big lug was crying. Openly, without shame, he was letting the tears run down his cheeks. He did try to control his sobs but only enough to let him get his words out.

When he did get them out, though, they were peculiar. He kept talking about it, not about him. Sicilian dialect has its oddities, but I'd never before run into anything like this confusion of pronouns.

"Where is he?" I asked.

"What do you want with him?"

"That's a stupid question. I want to take him back to his sister."

"For the three million? Of course, like with Rocco and Simone."

"Who are Rocco and Simone?"

"They had the bag. You took it from them. Like Chicago."

"In *Napoli?* The two kids on the motorcycle?"

"Yes. Rocco and Simone. They passed the word. Everybody knows. The American hijacker."

Things were beginning to clear. It wasn't Cathy they'd been keeping under surveillance. It was Matthew Erridge, the American hijacker. He had to be watched because he would do them as he had done Rocco and Simone. Furthermore, he was obviously still at it. Hadn't he back in Naples hijacked the coolie bag at the point of a gun? Now here he was again with gun in hand.

"I didn't keep the bag or anything in it. I took it all back to Miss Martin."

"Yes. Mr. Martin, he told us. You gave back the little money to get in for taking the big."

"Mr. Martin told you that?"

"He said you gave her back the bag with the money. We told him you were the American hijacker, but he didn't believe us."

"Where have you got him?"

"In the house."

"Where's the house?"

"Make a deal?"

"What's the deal?"

"I'll help you hijack Mr. Martin away from Jack. You'll have him all for yourself for the whole three million, but you help me get Vittorio away from Jack."

"Who's Vittorio?"

I was making a guess on Jack. He would be the American we had seen in Naples, the thug in the wild Paisley jacket. The notes would obviously be his work, and he was the one who hadn't shown anywhere since. It worked out. He was running the racket and he was sending his boys out to take all the risks.

Vittorio was different. He had me stopped. The only way I could figure this thing was that they were running two kidnappings at once. This guy was offering to split with me. Between us we'd cut Jack out of the whole deal and between us we'd whack up the spoils. The Martin ransom for me and the ransom for this Vittorio to Curly Top. Unless Vittorio was as good a prospect as Hugh Martin, he was asking for the same kind of split as I'd given those kids back in Naples. I take the big bread and I let him have a crumb.

"You don't get Vittorio, no part of him," he sobbed.

Now he was crying again.

I was tempted to tell him that I didn't want any part of Vittorio, but then I couldn't say it. Vittorio could have a sister somewhere. Okay. She could hardly be as beautiful as Cathy Martin, since there are too few who come that beautiful, but even an ugly woman can be in agony.

"Who is he?" I repeated.

"Why do you want to know?"

"I never go into any deal blind."

"Vittorio is my brother."

"I saw him with you in Naples?"

"We were always together."

"Where is he?"

"In the house."

He wants to hold his own brother for ransom? Is this nut going to be an asset or a liability?

"What are you going to do with the ear?"

That started the tears and the sobs again.

"You can't have it. I won't give it to you. You can kill me."

A nut with a thing for ears. This was just what I needed, but Huddles was in the house and this crazy idiot knew the way to the house. I hadn't the first thought of what I could do with him. There was just the one thing I knew. I couldn't do without him.

"You can keep the ear. I want the rest of him, and I want him alive and well."

The sobs came under control and the tears dried up. They were replaced by a crafty look. Abruptly he was no longer looking me in the eye.

"Alive?" he asked.

"He won't be any good to me dead."

"Put your gun away. It's a deal."

IX.

I shoved the gun back into my belt and he climbed out of Tiny Tin. I didn't like this new look he was wearing. We were standing full in the beam of Baby's headlights. I'd wanted it that way so I could see his every move. It also let me watch his every change of expression.

Stowing the gun, I was taking a calculated risk. We'd made a deal and I saw no way I could go on with him unless I acted as though I believed it, but this guy wasn't easy to believe. That he gave every evidence of being crazy had become the least of it. Now he had taken on the appearance of a guy who's just discovered a way he can pull a double-cross. A double-cross could be bad enough. I couldn't begin to understand what a crazy double-cross might be.

He was big. He was young. He was strong. Just on the way he came out of the car, if not on the way he had taken me in the shrubbery back at the hotel, he was obviously a guy who knew how to handle himself. In the mean art of dirty fighting, he would be an able practitioner if not even a man of accomplishment.

Holding myself ready for anything, I offered him my hand. I was deliberately giving him what he could take as an opening. It's an old trick but a good one. You're shaking a man's hand. You have him off guard and you also have possession of his right. You take a good grip and you keep possession. A zinging left? A quick knee to the groin? You can be more than halfway toward taking your man.

He took my hand and he shook it. That look of stealthy calculation left him, but I had no way of knowing what was replacing it. It had gone perhaps only because it couldn't coexist with sobs and tears. Yes, Charlie, he was crying again. He let go of my hand and he took a step closer to me. I was watching for anything he might try, and when he came in close that way, I was watching particularly for the knee.

But he didn't try anything. He threw his arms around me and hauled me close up against him in a tight hug. Dropping his face to my shoulder and hanging on tight, he had a good cry all over me. You may recall that earlier that night I had wanted just this from Cathy, but this wasn't the same. I was just getting wet. I could have picked up as big a charge from standing around in the rain.

With his face burrowed down into my shoulder I had no way of knowing whether what was raining down on me would be tears of joy or tears of grief. Even if I could have been seeing his face, I doubt that I could have known. Tears are tears. They don't come with labels on them.

For the moment there wasn't much I could do but play along, making the suitable gestures and the suitable noises. I patted his shoulder. I muttered what I hoped might be an Italian equivalent of "there, there." I urged him to pull himself together. I reminded him that we had work to do and that time was wasting. After not too long I could begin to sense some signs of a change in climate. The storm was dwindling down to a drizzle. Sobs were disintegrating into mere sniffles.

Taking that for the strategic time, I handed him one of

those let's-go-boys-time-to-get-in-there-and-fight smacks on
the butt. Football coaches seem to have great faith in the
procedure. If it works on linebackers, why shouldn't it be
equally effective on other varieties of muscle mass?

It seemed to work. I think it helped dry him up. He
pulled away from me and took a quick look at the gun in
my belt.

"You have a gun for me?" he asked.

I told him I didn't carry spares.

He frowned.

"He has two guns, one like yours but also a tommy."

There was nothing I could do about that. I like to travel
light. No submachine guns in my luggage.

"Who?" I asked.

"Jack."

"American? Not big, but heavy and strong?"

"Strong?" My new-found partner in crime was disdainful. "Vittorio could tear him apart and eat him for breakfast. His guns make him strong."

"In Naples he kept Martin in girls?"

"In Naples. In Agrigento."

"With promises that there would be better ones first in
Taormina and then in Palermo."

"Taormina he promised, yes, but not Palermo. Here."

"Okay. Who's in the house?"

"Jack, Martin, Vittorio."

"Women?"

"No women. Here they were only a promise. He never
had them here."

"So it's Jack alone standing guard on Martin and your
brother. He has nobody to back him up?"

"He has guns to back him up."

"He can use only one of them at a time if he has nobody
to work the extra gun."

"He thinks he has me."

"Is he wrong?"

"He is wrong."

"He had you. He had you for a long time."

"He had me and Vittorio. Me alone he'll never have. Vittorio is my brother."

"If you're not his man any more, why did you take her the ear and why did you take it back?"

"He made me do it. He would be angry if I didn't. He's terrible when he's angry. He's terrible with his guns."

"He told you to take the ear to her. He didn't tell you to bring it back?"

"He told me to bring it to her, and he told me I had to steal it back. He didn't know that when I stole it back it wouldn't be for him. I was never going to let him have it, not him or anyone else, but now he is going to know."

I couldn't believe a word of that. One nut with a thing for ears put a strain on my credulity. The possibility that there could be two of them and both ready to kill for the ear and even to die for it shattered all possible belief.

"If you and I go in to take him," I asked, "can we look for any help from Martin or your brother?"

"How can they help us when they can't even help themselves?"

"He has his guns on them. They can't do anything, not in the face of his guns. Say we come in on him. He has to turn his guns on us. Can we hope that they would jump him then?"

"He has Signor Martin tied up and locked in a room."

"And Vittorio?"

That question set him off again. More tears, more sobs. Past all the gulps and the sniffles it wasn't easy to catch what he was trying to say. It sounded as though he might have been trying to tell me that Vittorio could do nothing, but I did get the guts of the message. We could hope for nothing from Vittorio.

It hit me that there might be a clue to all those tears. Brother Vittorio had been to the test and had proved out for not as much man as my lachrymose pal had supposed him to be. Overcome with grief, he was still out to do what he must. Blood was thicker than water and there was family honor to be retrieved or something like that.

I changed the subject in the hope that any diversion might serve to stop the flow.

"You call me Matt," I said. "What's your name?"

"Ercole."

Victory and Hercules—common enough names in Italy. I don't know that people often think of what the names mean when they slap them on a baby boy. If there had been any such thinking done about this pair, it seemed to me that it had to be parental hopes gone unrealized. After all, Charlie, this weeping willow and what was sounding more and more like a coward.

It was no good wanting things different. I was going to have to make my move with what I had.

"Jack's expecting you back?"

"Yes."

"With the ear?"

"Yes, but I'm not going to give it to him."

"Even if he's angry with the terrible anger of his guns?"

"He can kill me."

It was a permission he seemed to be throwing out in all directions.

"You weren't going back to the house just to get killed?"

"I was going back to wait till Jack goes to pick up the three million. I can get Vittorio out of there then."

"Vittorio and the ear?"

"Vittorio and everything. I thought maybe if I watched

for it, he might give me a chance before that, before it would be anything more than the ears."

I've always thought I had a good, strong stomach. There aren't many things you can tell me that will pick my gut up and turn it inside out, but Ercole had found a way. The ear had been only the first installment. If Cathy couldn't get that three million in ransom to him as fast as he would like it, he was planning to nudge her along by sending her other hacked off pieces of Huddles. He had intimated as much in his message on the candy box, but now this was something more.

Nobody's going to tell me that in itself it wasn't a Grade-A, triple-plated stomach turner, but now I had Ercole as well. Already passionately attached to the severed ear, he was hell bent on collecting anything else that terrible Jack would get around to lopping off.

What I couldn't understand was why, if he was so hooked on collecting anatomical bits and pieces, he should prefer to make off with brother Vittorio and the ear at a time when for his purposes it would be so premature that he would have nothing for his collection but the ear.

I was careful to ask no questions about that. Why would I risk putting any ideas of waiting into his curly head when even the immediate removal of Hugh Martin from Jack's bloody hands was already too late by at least one ear?

"Where has he got them?" I asked. "Where's the house?"

"We passed a side road a little before this?"

"Yes. I saw it."

He explained that the house was up that first road but well along it. Taking that road, we would first come to a village. He put the distance to the village at about five to six kilometers, and then it would be another five kilometers beyond the village to the house.

I didn't have to ask him why he had stopped where he

did. He went right on into an explanation of that without any prodding or prompting from me. I'd had the tail on him and on the *autostrada* when he'd doused his lights and ridden the last few kilometers dark, he had been trying the only trick he could think of to lose me. Sucking me into the bushes back at the hotel had been his first trick. When that one hadn't worked, his spirit had broken. He had tried the trick of riding without lights only with the thought of leaving no stone unturned. He'd never expected it would work, not against a man who was so closely in league with the devil that Satan will sit up there giving him traffic directions from a brimstone-fueled helicopter.

He could think of no other way by which I could have known that he would be taking the Palermo-Catania *autostrada* or any way by which I could have picked up the further information that told me he would be driving Tiny Tin.

I didn't enlighten him. The best hope I could have would be that he might fear me even more than he feared Terrible Jack and his angry guns. Against that competition, I could do all right only as long as Ercole continued thinking of me as Mighty Matt and his ally, the Devil.

So when on the mountain road I turned up on his tail again, it had been no more than he'd been expecting. He had to face it. There would be no shedding me. So there he was. He had a choice of unpromising alternatives, and he had chosen the one that seemed the least likely to lead to his quick demise. He hadn't seen much hope that it, too, would not be fatal; but, having no good bet, he'd settled for the best of a bad lot.

This American hijacker, Erridge, had made a deal with those motorcycle kids back in Naples. It hadn't been any great deal for them, but they'd come out of it with whole skins, and you'll never find the Italian who'll knock that.

Italians believe in life. Of course, the way I'd seen it, I hadn't given those kids any kind of a deal at all, a bit of largesse, but no deal. It was only to have been expected, however, that in passing the word, the kids had built it up into a deal. A guy can lose face even if he isn't an Oriental, and Naples, after all, has been called the westernmost city of the Orient.

The only alternative Ercole had seen for himself was that he go on to the house with Baby's nose nudging him all the way. He couldn't read that for anything but dead on arrival. Picture it for yourself.

He would tool Tiny Tin up to the door with Baby hard behind him. Where does that put him? It puts him sandwiched between the two American savages, Terrible Jack and his guns and Mighty Matt with his gun and his Satanic alliance. Caught in the field of fire Ercole would die, and it would be of nothing but having been in the wrong place.

Failing his dying that way, of course, he would be gunned down by Jack. Jack didn't tolerate mistakes. He didn't tolerate failure. To have guided Erridge and the Devil straight to the house would surely have been rated as the inexcusable blunder.

"That's not the way it's going to be," I told him. "I won't be following you. I'll be riding with you."

He crossed himself, an elementary precaution. Riding with Erridge would mean riding with the Devil as well. A man can be expected to take only so much risk without even so standard a precaution as the sign of the Cross.

"In your beautiful car? He'll shoot us both as soon as we come into sight."

"In your beautiful car," I said.

He looked at me bug-eyed and then he looked at Baby.

"You'll abandon that?" he asked.

We were coming up even. He was developing doubts of my sanity which were easily the equal of my doubts of his.

"I'll leave it here. We'll come back for it later."

"The birds will dirty it."

"Better for the birds to bomb it than for Jack to bounce bullets off it."

Meanwhile, however, the two of us went and sat in Baby. She has a good dashboard light and I needed it if I was going to draw floor plans. I found some unmailed letters Cathy had written. They were in the glove compartment. They had been waiting for mailing when the Post Office strike would be over. The backs of the envelopes would do fine and Cathy could address fresh ones if the mails ever moved again.

"The road to the house?" I asked. "How close can we come before he'll see the lights of your car?"

"A kilometer away," he said, "and about half as far as from here to where we turned off."

A kilometer on one hand and about fifty yards on the other? I needed a better answer than that.

"It can't be both," I said.

But it could. He explained. On our approach to the house we would be coming along a mountain side. About a kilometer away by road, but much less than that as the crow flies, we would be in plain view of the house across the valley as we passed along the mountainside. Coming off the mountain and making its turn toward the house, however, the road disappeared into thick growths and anything passing along it could not again be seen from the house until it was within about fifty yards.

Having so sane an explanation out of him made me feel better.

"Does the road go anywhere else or just to the house?" I asked. "When he sees something on the road across the valley, does he know it's coming to him or can it be going farther along the road?"

Farther along the road there wasn't much. What few places there were beyond the house had no automobiles coming to them. If anything came along the road and went on past the house, it would be only a donkey cart.

"When he sees something across the valley, he gets ready with his guns," Ercole said. "He's waiting when it comes into sight near the house."

"Do you know another place like this, a place nearer the house where I can leave my car?"

"Like this. Off the road. In the woods. It's a good place and near the house."

"How near?"

"A hundred meters, a hundred and fifty at the most. But he'll see you when you pass along the road across the valley. It's after that."

He was, of course, exaggerating the formidable Jack's powers just as he tended to exaggerate mine. I was taking his impressions of the situation and whittling them down to something nearer life size.

Obviously, if this Jack was holding two men prisoners and he had to stand guard over them alone, he could hardly spend all his time with his eyes glued to that short stretch of road across the valley. Still it was better to overestimate the man than to underestimate him. He would be waiting for Ercole's return. He would be watching for him. I couldn't count on passing by during a moment when he might blink and miss me.

"You will tell me when we're near the part of the road he can see from across the valley. I'll do that stretch without lights. I can do it following you."

"Good," he said. "Much better place to leave this, a safer place."

Maybe he thought the birds were more continent in this other place. I wasn't asking. He was stroking the Porsche's upholstery. I was wondering whether any woman had ever had from his hand as loving a touch.

I left it at that. It was better than telling him I preferred not to put too much reliance on him and Tiny Tin. I moved on to asking him about the house. That was rougher going than the road. I went through several envelope backs before I had drawn up from his answers to my questions a floor plan in which I could feel any confidence. The house had only one door. It had three rooms, a large front room that was everything and two small back rooms that were nothing, except that Jack had found a use for them. He had a trussed-up Huddles locked up in one of them and he had Vittorio locked away in the other.

You may think there could hardly have been a simpler floor plan, but when you want to know what I needed to know, stuff like exact placement of doors and windows, and you are doing it out of the memory of someone who isn't floor-plan minded, it gets to be more than a little hairy.

Take, for example, getting straightened out on which captive was in which room. I did all I could to make it easy for him. I asked him to imagine himself coming in the front door. Would he have the doors to the back rooms facing him?

"No."

"Then where are they?"

"On the wall across from the front door."

"Then they would be facing you."

"No."

I drew that much of it for him and asked him to show me where the doors should go. After much study he indicated their positions. The places he indicated were the places where he'd just said the doors wouldn't be. I could have left it there, but it was too important that I should be sure I had it right.

After too much discussion I was finally able to relax on that piece of it. To him opposite meant directly across and in line with the front door, not across and off to right and left.

Then came the question of which captive was in which room. We had another considerable go around on which was right and which left. Step by step I had to try to pin him down to which way he was looking at the two rooms and he just couldn't do it in his head. When I asked him to indicate it on the floor plan, he got even more confused.

I finally worked it by hauling out of the car with him and standing him bellied up against the Porsche's door. He had the hood to the right of him and the trunk to the left. Then I asked him to think of the fenders on the other side of the car as the two rooms. In which one was Huddles, in which Vittorio? That did it.

Huddles was in the trunk. Vittorio was under the hood.

I marked them on my plan. Then we sweated out the windows, determining their exact placement. Most of that proved to be for nothing.

I must take the blame for that. Maybe if I'd told him why I wanted to know exactly what windows there were and where, he might have thought to tell me.

My last question was about Jack. Was he right-handed or left-handed. That one was easy. Ercole was more comfortable with people than he was with architecture.

Jack was right-handed.

It was lucky I'd thought to ask.

X.

We went out of there pretty much as we had come in. I wasn't following him as close as I had been, but I wasn't hanging back either. I was giving him a couple of car lengths lead on Baby but no more than that. I wasn't letting myself forget the crafty look that had suddenly come over him. He had thought of something that gave him a new lease on life, and he was giving me no clue to what that something might be.

It could be that somewhere on the road ahead he was remembering a place that would be just right for losing me, and that I was not going to let happen. I had come too long a way. Nobody was going to wash me out now. As we rode along, however, with Tiny Tin leading the way and me following after in Baby, the thought that he might make another try at losing me faded out. Another possibility presented itself. For a while there, when I had been setting it up for leaving the Porsche in the woods and riding the rest of the way with him, he had taken all too readily to that way of doing it.

He had shown some concern for Baby's safety and well being, but apart from that, he hadn't been sufficiently bothered by the prospect of taking me on as a passenger in Tiny Tin. If he'd had me in his car with him riding along at his side, how could he have hoped to lose me? That made no sense, not even Ercole's lunatic variety of sense.

It had to be something else, and there was only the one other thing I could think of. He would be carrying me into an ambush, but I couldn't quite make that one work either. On his description of the road, he'd had a perfect set up for an ambush and he'd thrown it away.

There was that stretch along the mountainside where we could be seen from the house across the valley. He needn't have told me about that. I would have driven it on his tail and never have known that I was being seen. Meanwhile, Jack, keeping watch, would see the lights of two cars where there should have been only one. He could have been alerted and waiting.

Driving along in Ercole's wake, I tried to come at it from every angle, but nothing was any better than anything else.

We passed through the village he had mentioned, a cluster of dark, sleeping houses and only one lighted window that I could see in the whole place. One solitary insomniac? A sick room? A couple of kilometers past the town he flickered his lights, giving me the signal. We were coming to that mountainside stretch. I doused my lights and let him pull ahead of me one extra car length. I was making certain that I would be holding far enough back so that if he slowed suddenly, there would be no chance of my drawing up close enough on him for even the dim red glow of his taillights to throw a gleam off Baby's bright work and even for a moment give me away.

But he ran that whole stretch behaving himself perfectly. He held to a steady speed. He never pulled anything sudden on me. Then we were drilling our way through a leafy tunnel. He flickered his lights again. It was his second signal. We were past the stretch where we might have been seen.

I switched Baby's lights on but not without wondering

whether I wasn't letting myself be suckered. Those flicker-ing-light signals had been Ercole's idea. Now I was wonder-ing whether they had really been as advertised. Had they been signals to me or signals to Jack? Was that stretch visi-ble from the house or was this the thing that had popped into Ercole's mind at that moment when he'd abruptly slid away from looking me in the eye? He had thought of a way he could signal Jack with his lights without rousing me to even the first trace of suspicion.

It was a possibility. It wouldn't be smart for me to disre-gard it. I couldn't even disregard the chance that it could be wishful thinking that was making me feel that I needn't worry about it. It seemed too clever. I just couldn't figure that Ercole, even in his right mind, could be a brain, and if I was convinced of anything that night, it was that Ercole wasn't in his right mind. He was all too evidently any place else but.

We left the road. He led me along a track that made ev-erything else we'd come over seem like superhighway, but in there he found a place wide enough so he could pull over and leave me room to pass him. He stopped and came over to Baby.

"You go ahead," he said. "Straight in. I have to be behind you so I can back out. You'll see Martin's car."

Straight in to what?

I opened the Porsche's door.

"You come with me. Show me the way."

With a growl of impatience he jumped in and pulled the door shut after him. He was careful not to slam it or even to put the little heft into it that would make the lock en-gage. He just kept his hand on the door, holding it shut. It was encouraging if he was being that careful not to make any sound that might carry to the house. He was whispering. I hadn't thought we were that close, but I followed his lead. I held myself down to a whisper, too.

"You must be quick," he said. "Jack knows how long it takes to drive around the other side of the valley. He will think something if I take too long."

If this was an act he was putting on, it was too good an act. I couldn't believe he had it in him. He was no kind of a con artist. He was just muscle. It was only a matter of a few yards and a turn in the track before we came on the Rolls. It looked strange in there but I guess Baby did as well, gleaming monsters out of another world. Only Tiny Tin could look at home here. It wasn't too far a reach from the donkey carts.

We left Baby with her doors hanging open, not risking even the click of the door latches. Walking back to Tiny Tin, I whispered final instructions. I would ride in with him crouched down in the back seat out of sight. I wanted him to pull up broadside to the house so that I could crawl out the far door and not be seen. He told me he could do better than that. He would stop as I suggested but with the far side of Tiny Tin tight against the bushes that edged the clearing in front of the house. I could crawl out and go straight into the concealment of the bushes.

I told him that would be great and asked him if I could count on such concealment all the way around to the back of the house. He said I would have it all the way to the window of the room where Huddles was tied up. I would have to cross a wide open space to get to the room where Jack had Vittorio.

"That's all right," I said. "Vittorio is yours."

"All mine," he whispered.

It's not easy to make a whisper sound emphatic, but Ercole managed it. He was making a point and it was important to him. I saw no reason to dispute him on that. I went on with the rest of what I wanted him to do.

"Go into the house with Jack," I said. "Tell him you delivered the ear. Tell him you waited outside her door and listened. Tell him you heard her scream and the thud of her body when she fell. Tell him you went into the room and found her out cold in a faint. Tell him you grabbed the ear and took off. Tell him you took so long because when you left the package at the desk, they didn't send it right up to the room. You had to wait and watch till finally a boy took it up. That'll take care of any questions he may have about why you've been so long. Complain about the bad service in such a de luxe hotel. Make a long story of it. Keep him busy as long as you can."

"That will help you," he said. "You will help me?"

"I'll come in and take him. Once I have him and I have his guns, you can start moving. Are you going to need more help than that?"

He gave me no direct answer but it was evident that he was ready to call it adequate help. He moved on to another question.

"Jack," he said. "You will take his guns away from him?"

"You do your part. I'll do mine."

"You'll take his guns, but you'll leave him for me. He'll be mine to kill?"

"You'll have Vittorio. Do you need him?"

"I need him to kill. With a knife. Slow."

I got the picture. Erridge holds a gun on the bastard while Ercole slices him up, down, and sideways. That's never been the game the way I played it, but I'd seen the ear and I could have sold myself on thinking that with this bastard, Jack, it was a game with different rules. What was stopping me was knowing myself. When it came right down to it, I'd never be able to make myself do it.

"We'll talk about that after I have his guns," I said. "First things first. You want Vittorio more, don't you?"

"Yes," he said. "Vittorio first."

I didn't want to think that it was to be a knife job on yellow-bellied brother as well, but I was going to have to take that on, too, when I came to it. It would be no good telling him now that any talking we were going to do about it would get nothing out of Erridge but no and no and no. Until I had the guns I needed his co-operation. At best I wasn't certain that I would have it. This could still be sucking me into an ambush, but if I was to have anything from him, I couldn't spoil it now.

So we left it at that. I stowed myself in the back, crouched down on the floor so that no part of me showed. It was a tight squeeze since Tiny Tin offered only the dead minimum of crouching room, but I made it.

Ercole climbed in behind the wheel and took off. Only after he had the car in motion did I haul the gun out of my belt and hold it at the ready. At the first move he might make that wasn't included in our agreed program I was prepared to start shooting. Whether the first slug would be for Jack or for Ercole would depend on the circumstances. I knew my own plan, but I was riding along on it with every expectation that it was going to go awry. Whether it would be through betrayal or simple bad luck when it came, I was going to be ready to come up with whatever improvisation might be necessary.

We were riding into battle and I was going armed with my battle plan. Doing what you intend to do is always only part of it. You must be prepared as well to cope with the unknown—the tricks of chance and the enemy's battle plan.

So far as I could determine, Ercole was playing it straight. He drove back out to the road. He turned in the expected direction. He did only one thing of which I hadn't been forewarned. That came when I estimated he had driven a little more than half the distance he'd said we'd have to cover before we'd pull up at the house.

He sounded the horn. I couldn't take the risk of rising up to see whether he was shooing some chickens or a goat or a deer off the road, but such risk was also unnecessary. For shooing animals out of your path you don't play tunes on your horn. Two toots, a pause, three toots. The pattern was unmistakable, and I had ample opportunity for checking it out.

He kept repeating it throughout the rest of the run all the way to the place where he pulled up. Even after he'd come to a stop, he sat in the car and worked the horn. Two blasts, a pause, three blasts. It was a signal. It could never have been anything else. In all likelihood it was nothing I needed to worry about. The fact that he hadn't said a word about it was disturbing, but the best bet was to assume that warning me of it had just slipped his mind.

To think that he could have had any purpose in keeping it from me was to think more out of fright than out of reason. A guy has to drive into the face of a revolver and a submachine gun, and both weapons in the hands of a ruthless, trigger-happy sonofabitch. He'd be crazy to do it without some prearranged signal, some way of announcing his arrival and saying: "Put the guns away. It's only your faithful Ercole."

If he had told me about it, wouldn't I have accepted it without suspicion? Or would I? That there should have been a signal made sense, but what was to say that there hadn't been a variety of signals—one that would tell Jack to relax it's only Ercole; another pattern of hoots to tell him to take to the hills because Ercole was coming in with the fuzz on his tail; yet another to indicate that Ercole was coming but only under duress as the captive of the American hijacker?

I didn't wait to find out. I slithered out of the back of the car and drilled my way well into the bushes while Ercole was still waiting behind the wheel and nothing had yet shown from the house. I was better off in the bushes. I could peer through them and see something of what was going on. It was not an unimpeded view but it was better than anything I could have had crouched down in the car.

The front of the house was as advertised. Position of the door and placement of the windows were so close to the way we'd finally pinned them down on my floor plan as could make no difference.

The door opened but only a crack just wide enough to permit the passage of the tommy-gun muzzle. Quickly Ercole sounded his horn signal again. Obviously, he had been through one of these homecomings before. In pulling to his stop he had put himself in a place where the gun could not be brought to bear on him unless the door was thrown wide.

It didn't happen. The door was held to the crack. Nothing showed but the machine-gun barrel.

A voice came from behind the door.

"Erk?"

"Yes, Jack. Ercole. Who else?"

"You got it to her?"

"I did it the way you said. I left it at the hotel desk. I watched the clerk put it in the box for the letters. The number was on the box. I went up and waited outside her room."

"And the rest of it? You did the rest of it?"

"I didn't have to knock her out. She fainted."

"That's even better. You brought it back anyhow."

"I took it away from her."

"Okay. Come on in."

That should have been the moment. It stood as opportunity No. 1 in the battle plan. He would throw the door wide and hold it open while Ercole got out of the car and came to the door. I'd have a clear field of fire and from my concealment in the bushes I'd take careful aim to put a slug into him. I was planning on the right arm or the right shoulder. No need to try for as small and chancy a target as his shooting hand.

There could be no question but that this was the man I wanted. It wasn't Vittorio. It was Jack himself. I didn't have to depend on having heard Ercole call him Jack. I knew the voice. I had heard it that time in the Naples night club, and past the phony accent I had heard it on the telephone. Now he would be mine for the taking.

But he wasn't. He didn't throw the door wide to welcome his faithful retainer. He didn't stand in the doorway silhouetted against the light and offering an easy target.

He hauled the tommy gun back in and shut the door. Not the smallest part of him had shown in the whole process. He was leaving it to Ercole to go over and open the door for himself. He had pulled back.

Reluctant to give up on my No. 1 plan of attack, I waited until Ercole was out of the car and over to the door. When he opened it, Jack might still be waiting just inside the doorway to welcome him. Whether I could get my shot in then was doubtful. I would have to take the chancy shot past Ercole, and I couldn't afford to miss or to send a slug into the wrong man. As long as there was the slightest possibility that he would present a good target, however, I had to stick with it. I wasn't going into this so rich in chances that I could let myself pass anything up.

Ercole opened the door. Jack was nowhere in sight. Ercole went in and shut the door behind him. It was time to
put my first alternative into operation. Keeping myself deep
in the shrubbery, I made a wide sweep around to the back
of the house. The concealment was great all the way
around to the window of the room where Ercole had said
Jack was keeping Huddles. I could see beyond to the window of the room where Ercole said we'd find Vittorio and
there was no gap in the concealing underbrush.

I tried to figure why Ercole would have lied to me about
that one detail. I couldn't see how it would be important
but, just as evidence that he hadn't leveled with me all the
way, it was there to bug me.

That, however, was the least of it. I had something else
and it was bugging me a lot more. The window was exactly
where on Ercole's information I had placed it in the floor
plan. He hadn't screwed me up on that. There I had to take
the credit. I'd screwed myself up. Since I hadn't thought to
ask him and since I hadn't told him why I needed to know,
I couldn't gripe about his not having told me.

The window was where he'd put it, but it wasn't the window I'd expected it to be.

Out front and at the side of the house, where the windows gave on the front room, they weren't enormous windows but they were decently generous. At the back the
windows that gave on the two back rooms were hardly
worth the name. They were no more than little holes in the
wall.

Climbing in, cutting Huddles loose, moving him safely
out of the line of fire, and then crashing the locked door to
burst into the front room with gun blazing to take the
enemy from the rear, such had been the first alternative
battle plan, and now that was down the drain along with
No. 1. If I'd had a small boy with me, I could have boosted

him through that window, but it would need to have been a very small boy.

I pulled myself up to that pathetic excuse for a window and I got myself to a place where I had the window sill securely wedged in my left armpit. Hanging there that way, I tried to see in. It wasn't the darkest of nights out in the open. There was a good moon and a lot of stars—enough light for the comfortable execution of night maneuvers.

Inside that room, though, it looked like total blackness. After I had been staring into it for a while—it seemed a couple of lifetimes, but it couldn't have been nearly that much—I began to adjust and I made out a lighter blur in the surrounding black. That would have to be Huddles lying trussed up on the floor. After another interval of looking hard the blur took on something like a human shape. I found myself belatedly admiring the Martin taste in clothes, lots of whites, those expensively bleach-stained blue jeans, are light-colored stuff. If he had been wearing black, I could never have found him.

Still hanging from that window sill and working one-handed, I shoved the gun into my belt and fished my pocketknife out of my pants pocket.

Where I was could never be mistaken for a pitcher's mound, but taking the best aim I could, I pitched the knife at the blur that had to be Huddles. My markmanship was good but my thinking had been lousy. I lobbed it neatly onto him where he was lying, but all it did was startle him. I saw the blur heave up and I heard it give out with one of those half articulate sounds a sleeping man will make when he comes only half awake.

The knife rolled off him and dropped to the floor. I heard it hit. I wanted to call to him, but I couldn't risk the noise. If it had been a proper window or even that little one not placed so high in the wall, noise could have been just what I needed.

Huddles starts shouting and acting up. Jack comes back to silence him. He opens the door from the lighted front room. It could be as good as what I'd been disappointed of out front, the amount of perfect target when he would be silhouetted against the light in the doorway.

I played with the idea. Hanging up there in the window sill, I pulled the gun back out of my belt. I made a try at raising it and aiming it at the place where my floor plan said the door should have been. It was no good. I'd be working within too restricted an arc of fire and, hanging the way I was, I couldn't hold anything like a steady aim.

I dropped back to the ground and none too soon. If I'd hung there much longer, I'd have had myself fixed for going into whatever action I was still hoping to find under the handicap of a useless left arm.

I worked my way back around the house, but out front I had to give up on my concealment. I needed to come up close to one of the front windows and that was impossible without crossing the clearing in front of the house. There was nothing for it. I was down to the last poor alternative of my battle plan. I was out in the relative darkness. He was in the lighted room. I was wishing for a nice thick cloud to come along and wrap up the moon, but that was hopeless. From horizon to horizon the stars were twinkling. It was one of those great Sicilian skies, free of even the first wisp of cloud.

I had to move in slowly, offering nothing sudden to catch his eye, close enough to see but not so close that the light from the window would fall on me. They were talking. I could hear their voices, but they were holding it too low for me to make out the words, except that the sound was angry.

As I came in closer, I could hear the anger grow. They were bringing their voices up and at the same time my ears were tuning in. When I had moved up close enough to see in, I held it there. What I could see, however, was only part of the room. Right up against the open window I could have looked in on all of it but not without myself being seen.

I could see Ercole but I could only hear Jack. No part of him was in my line of sight. Ercole was crying again. They were going on and on about the ear. Ercole was calling on the Holy Mother and the whole calendar of saints to bear witness that he had left the ear with Cathy only long enough for her to have seen it. He swore that he had taken it away with him but he was also swearing that he hadn't brought it back with him. He had taken it away from Cathy, but he had deposited it in a safe place.

Jack was calling him a liar. He was warning him of what would happen to him if he didn't come up with the ear.

"You can't have it," Ercole sobbed. "It's mine."

"You're crazy. You're a crazy liar. You saw what I did to Vittorio."

"Vittorio didn't lie to you. How could he know they weren't diamonds? When you saw them, you didn't know."

"I didn't know. How could anybody know? When he came back with the money and it wasn't enough, how could I know he wasn't lying? It was his fault anyhow, grabbing the junk and leaving the real stuff."

"It was a mistake. Anybody could make such a mistake."

"Okay. It was a mistake and now you're making a mistake. I don't hold still for mistakes."

He didn't hold still for them but he did make them. I must admit, though, that Ercole triggered it. Ercole made his mistake first.

"You can kill me," he said, "but I won't give it to you."

That wasn't his mistake. That was a safe enough invitation. It was obvious that Jack couldn't afford to kill him. Jack still needed him. Once Jack would have collected the ransom and been off to North Africa, he would be in a position to go it alone, but until then he would need Ercole. He was already badly shorthanded, down to only one man.

As Ercole spoke, however, the dope's hand moved to his pocket. Have you ever been in a crowded place and somebody jostles you? Automatically, without thinking, you put your hand on your pocket, feeling for your wallet, checking on whether it's still with you. People do that all the time, and pickpockets watch for it.

I saw Ercole's hand move and I wondered whether Jack would read it. He did. Maybe he'd never picked pockets, but he evidently knew the game. He had a pick-pocket's eye. It was only a turn of phrase that passed through my mind, but in passing it bugged me. These were cats who collected ears.

He moved in on Ercole and that brought him into my line of vision. He wasn't wearing the crazy jacket, but I didn't need it. I knew him without it. It was then that he made his mistake. He came at Ercole with his revolver. He had evidently left the tommy gun back in that part of the room I couldn't see, but obviously he couldn't use even the revolver.

Holding the gun on Ercole, he reached for the pocket. He was going to take the ear away from Ercole at gun point. Now, holding a gun on a desperate man will often enough get you nowhere. Make it a desperate man who knows you can't afford to shoot him, and you are likely to find yourself with nothing going for you.

Ercole ignored the gun. Grabbing Jack by the wrist, he caught him before he could touch the pocket. He could just as well have gone the rest of the way. He had Jack where he could have taken him, and even if it turned out that he couldn't, he was a cinch to have kept Jack tied up till I could come in and lend a hand.

Don't ask me why the imbecile didn't do it. It could have been because he was an imbecile, or he could have been thinking that, pushed far enough, Jack might lose his head and forget the main event long enough to squeeze the trigger.

So there they were flailing around with Ercole hanging on to Jack's wrist and Jack trying to break away and get to the pocket. I had them right there in front of me, but in all their silly wrestling they weren't turning to where I could get a clear shot at Jack. He was on the far side of Ercole. If I fired, there wasn't a prayer I wouldn't hit the wrong man.

They were so closely matched that they could have gone on through the rest of the night. I was beginning to think they would do just that, but then Jack made his move. He had the revolver in his right hand and that was his free hand. Ercole had a firm grip on Jack's left. Jack flung his right arm out and flipped the revolver into the air, catching it by the muzzle as it came down. It was a neat trick and neatly executed, but it was obvious that he wasn't doing it to show off. Since he couldn't allow himself to shoot Ercole, he was getting into position for clunking the idiot on his curly head with the gun butt.

Doing that trick close in on Ercole was impossible. He had to make a long stretch to the right. He couldn't know, of course, that in the doing he was giving me a clear line on his right shoulder.

I fired. The revolver he had just caught dropped from his hand and the impact of the slug in his shoulder would have knocked him on his ass if it hadn't been for Ercole's tight grip on the man's left wrist. He sagged, but with Ercole hanging on to him, he went down only to his knees. I didn't stay at the window to watch. I ran to the door and burst into the room.

Nothing much had changed. Jack was now on the floor at Ercole's feet. Since Ercole had let go of him and let him drop, Jack now had his left hand free for grabbing at his wounded shoulder. Ercole was standing over him looking stupid. I ran over and grabbed up the revolver from where it lay only inches away from Jack's right hand. He hadn't even tried for a left-handed pick up on it. All the fight had gone out of him, but he was still straight poison even if now it wasn't showing anywhere but in his eyes.

I looked around for the tommy gun. It was over at the far end of the room, nowhere he could make a grab at it even in the event that he might now come up ambidextrous. I grabbed him by his good arm and yanked him to his feet. Pushing him along ahead of me, I made for the door to the back room where he had Huddles locked up. I'd been expecting that I would have to make him cough up the key, but it was easier than that. The door wasn't locked. It was bolted. I pulled the bolt and, kicking the door open, I shoved him into the room ahead of me.

By the light from the front room I could see Huddles. His hands were tied behind his back and he was tied at the ankles. He was awake. He had to be. Even if he had dropped back to sleep after I'd lobbed the knife at him, he would have wakened when Ercole and Jack got to shouting at each other or, if not then, certainly by the shot.

I shoved Jack back against the far wall where the light from the front room fell full on him and I could watch his every move. There was nothing to watch. He wasn't moving. My knife was on the floor. I picked it up and worked at flipping the blade open. It took longer than the telling because I was doing it one-handed and blind, keeping both the gun and my eyes trained on Jack. I don't carry a switchblade, but that was one time I wished I did. My simple pocketknife had always served my purposes, but in that situation it was a pain in the ass.

After a lot of fumbling I had it open. I took my chances on Jack only just long enough to cut Huddles' hands free. In that moment Jack did make a small try. He slid over toward the darker part of that little back room, but he didn't get far before I had the gun on him again and I moved him back into the light.

His hands freed, Huddles took the knife out of my hand. He took care of freeing his ankles and immediately he tried to stand. Of course, he couldn't make it. It takes a little time to get the circulation going, and he was going to have to do some limbering up before he'd have his leg muscles unkinked enough to make them do what he wanted them to do.

"My legs," he said. "I'll be all right in a minute."

"Take your time."

"You think I'm a jerk."

"I think you're a jerk."

"And you're right. I am."

"I'm right. You are."

We could have gone on that way indefinitely, but suddenly something hit me. Something was not at all the way it had to be. I would probably have come up with it sooner if I'd been free to give full attention to looking Huddles over, or maybe even if I'd just had him in a better light. Half noticing, I looked harder and all that would come into my mind was a riddle kids used to ask.

"How many ears did Daniel Boone have?"

"Two."

"Wrong. He had three, a right ear, a left ear, and a wild front ear."

Dig, Charlie? A wild frontier.

Believe it or not, there was Huddles with both his right ear and his left ear attached and intact. So what about the one Ercole was going to cherish even at the risk of death? A wild front ear?

Huddles caught the way I was staring at him. I was rocked so hard by his two ears that I almost forgot Jack. He slid along the wall and, out of the path of light, he tried for the door. Huddles, still on the floor, shoved himself into Jack's path and tripped him. That woke me up. I resumed control. Riddles are only riddles. I wasn't going to let that bastard get behind me, not even when he had only the one working arm.

"The way you were looking at me," Huddles said. "Something wrong with me apart from my being a jerk?"

"Something's right with you and it shouldn't be. You've got an ear too many."

I explained about Ercole and the gruesome package he had delivered to Cathy. There was time for it. We were waiting for his legs to come back to the place where he could get some adequate use out of them. He couldn't explain it. All he knew was that Jack had provided him with a string of great parties and had promised the greatest party ever in Taormina. Then without any explanation that night in Agrigento Jack had run out on him.

At Siracusa during the evening in the old city Ercole had picked him up and told him that all bets were off for Taormina but that the party was still on. Jack had moved it to a house in the country where they would be away from everything, and it could be the greatest and the wildest. Huddles was to take the Catania-Palermo *autostrada*, leave it at the first exit after the Caltinasetta turnoff, drive on to the town, and they would meet him there to take him to he house.

"Acually they weren't waiting for me in the town," Huddles said. "They met me along the road after I left the *autostrada* and before I reached the town. Jack switched over to ride with me and Ercole followed in their car. It was all the way it had been right along till we got here to the house. This didn't look like any party place to me and I asked him where the girls were."

"You didn't suspect anything up to then?" I asked.

"No. It had all been fun and this was going to be more of the same, but better and wilder."

"You never thought to wonder why these guys were working so hard to keep this great road show going for you?"

Huddles shrugged.

"I was paying for it. They were getting a free ride and making a good profit. Even when we got here and I did begin to wonder and I did ask, I wasn't thinking anything like kidnapping. It was just that with no girls I thought maybe it was going to be a queer do, and I didn't want any of that. You see, I'd seen this bastard and Ercole and Vittorio in action. I knew that they swing both ways."

And that was it. Jack hadn't waited for suspicion to grow. At the first question, he'd pulled his gun on Huddles and told him that from there on out it wasn't Huddles' party any more. It was his.

"He herded me back here," Huddles said. "He held the gun on me while Ercole tied me up and that's been it. I knew he was hitting Cuddles for ransom money, but that was all right. I'd been an idiot and it was going to cost me, but, God, this ear business."

We tried questioning Jack, but he wasn't talking. He didn't know anything about any ear. If I wasn't making the whole thing up, that had to be my game and Ercole's. He turned from me to remind Huddles that he had warned him about me. Huddles wasn't to think he was in the clear. Nothing was changed except that he, Jack, had been dealt out of the game. I was hijacking Huddles from him just as I had hijacked the coolie bag from the two kids back in Naples.

He was taking it philosophically. It was all in the game and nobody could ever say Jack wasn't a good loser.

"Okay, buddy," he said to me. "You've won. So now do me the way I'd have done you if this was the other way around. Get me to a doctor who'll keep his mouth shut."

"The police'll get you to a doctor," I told him.

"Don't give me that. You can't go to the fuzz any more than I can, and meanwhile I'm bleeding to death."

He was bleeding, but it wasn't arterial and it wasn't even very much. I saw no need to tell him so. He was one of those guys who aren't bothered by the sight of blood except that they can't stand the sight of their own. It suited me to let him worry. It wasn't even the smallest part of what I owed him for Cathy. Huddles got to his feet. He'd had all the recovery time he needed. His legs were holding.

We moved it out to the front room. I was going to make a try at questioning Ercole. He wasn't there and the door to the other back room stood open. The room was empty. Ercole had taken off and he had taken Vittorio with him. It figured, and I tried to tell myself it was wrong to be glad of it. I couldn't quite get that made. I was glad.

There was one other thing gone as well, the tommy gun. I couldn't be glad of that. I didn't like to think what that idiot pair might do with that kind of armament. I don't know whether I was more concerned about them or about the people they might use as their target. I could see it as just what they needed to move them into a new crime bracket, and I was pretty sure it would be at a level where they wouldn't know how to cope.

I told Huddles to pick up the one remaining weapon, Jack's revolver. So we had two guns trained on him when we started out of the house. Out there it was no surprise that Tiny Tin should also have been missing. There was nothing for it but to march Jack out to where I'd left the Porsche and where the Rolls had also been parked. It did occur to me that since there were two of them, it could well have been a car apiece, but then it would have to be Tiny Tin and the Rolls. The keys to Baby I had in my pocket. This, after all, was the other side of nowhere, but there are the times when I seem to be brighter than I know.

The walk was slow going. Jack was balky. He had to be prodded and kicked along. When we made it up that little side track, I found that I'd been half right in my guess. There were two cars in there but one of them was Tiny Tin. The other was Baby. Ercole and Vittorio had switched to the Rolls for their taking off.

Huddles couldn't have been less disturbed. One Rolls more or less. There were always more where that one came from, and hadn't Erridge just saved the Martins three million smackers?

We kicked Jack into the Porsche. I set it up for him to be riding up front with me. That way Huddles in the back seat could keep the gun trained on him and we'd have no nonsense.

Driving out, I was trying to get my priorities in line. The first thing was a phone to get the word to Cathy. There was the town we'd passed through on the way from the *autostrada*. There would be one there, certainly the one Jack had used for placing his ransom call. On the timing I knew he had been alone when he made that call. By then Ercole had been on his way to Palermo with the ear. Leaving Huddles and Vittorio tied up and locked up but unguarded, he wouldn't have gone far for the telephone, certainly no far-

ther than that town. No question but that there would be a
telephone there but how to find it in the sleeping town? I
tried to get it out of Jack, like where he'd phoned from
when he made the call to Cathy, but he wasn't talking at all
beyond telling me that he would talk only on one condition
and that would be when I got him to that doctor who
wouldn't.

I remembered the one lighted window I'd seen when Ercole and I passed through coming in. I had to hope it
would still be showing a light. Second priority was going to
be handing Jack over to the fuzz. I didn't care where the
carabinieri might want him. I was going to take him to
Palermo because Cathy was up there, and I wasn't going to
have her wait an extra second before she saw Huddles for
herself and saw him with his complete allotment of ears.

If they wanted to meet me somewhere along the road
and take the sonofa off my hands there, it was okay with
me, but I was making no detours.

We were still short of the town when we heard the shooting. It was up the road ahead of us and there was nothing
for it but to drive on toward it. It didn't last long and it was
followed by total silence. From the sound of it, it had been
a lot of weapons and of various types. I couldn't separate
the sounds enough to say for sure that tommy-gun firing
had been part of the mix, but it was not unlikely.

About ten minutes driving after that we came around a
turn and ran into blinding light. I heard the bark of the
order and rammed Baby into reverse. She was backing
around the turn when the first shots came at her. We were
ambushed and it was a question of how to go about calling
off an ambush. This was clearly a shoot first and talk later
situation, but with the fire power confronting us there was
little chance we could have a later. Once I had us backed

around out of sight the firing died down. I knew that was going to be no more than temporary.

"What now?" Huddles asked. "Shoot our way through?"

"Not through the *carabinieri*," I told him.

"How do you know they are?"

"The ungodly don't work under floodlights."

I turned to our prisoner.

"You tell him, Jack," I said. "Who should know better?"

He suggested that I do something to myself that I couldn't possibly do, not even if my hips were double-jointed, which they are not.

It didn't matter. I managed without his expertise. I herded Jack out of the car and I told Huddles to come along. Moving them to the side of the road, I pushed Jack down and held him flat to the road and told Huddles to get down flat beside him keep him covered.

I squatted down behind Baby and started shouting. I was trying to open up communications. If nothing else, to plant in their narrow-gauge, one-track minds the thought that they might want to take us alive. I had no guarantee that they wouldn't be laying a barrage down on us before they came around the turn to see who we were. I worked at shouting every peaceable word I could think of, and I brought it off. They came around to us with their floodlights and with their every gun at the ready, but they did hold their fire. They took us alive. They were the *carabinieri*.

If you're thinking I could have waited, that since they had obviously been on the way, I could have held back and let them come in and take Jack, think again, Charlie. They would have come in against Jack's tommy gun and nobody in the house would have come out alive. If I'd had any doubt of that, it would have been eliminated as soon as I saw the Rolls and Ercole and Vittorio. Ercole hadn't gotten off even one burst from the tommy gun, but the Rolls was scarred all over by gun fire and Ercole dead weighed maybe twice what he'd tipped the scales at alive. He had that much lead in him. Vittorio was also dead and he also had a great load of lead in him, but he was not nearly as newly dead and he was lacking both his ears. Those the fuzz had found in Ercole's pocket and one of them so cold that it had obviously been not long off the ice.

I began all this by telling you how great Italians are. In any other country I know we would have been held up at least the rest of the night, making statements, signing them, all that crap. I'm not trying to tell you there isn't paper work in Italy, but Italy is the place where paper work, like anything else that isn't fun, can always wait. The *carabinieri* had telephone-equipped cars and they let Huddles and me both get on to talk to Cathy.

Furthermore, it was practically no time before they had us back on the road to Palermo and with a siren-screaming police escort. Of course, I had to hold Baby down to their top speed, but that was considerably more than I could have done legally without them and one helluva lot more than anybody could ever have done through the early morning traffic in Palermo.

It was great coming home to Cathy. She kissed Huddles everywhere available but particularly on his ears. She had to be told everything and she didn't believe much of it. She was working on her own version, and it was Supererridge all the way. She kissed me where I like it best and that isn't on my ears.

I was able to give her the full rundown. The *carabinieri* had filled me in on the bit I couldn't work out for myself, and that was how they had found their way to that back road. Their locals had been wondering about the house.

Too much traffic was going that way all of a sudden and some of it too rich. In areas where the eyes are adjusted to donkey carts a Rolls-Royce is more than notice-able.

They had, of course, been tipped by the switchboard operator to the content of Cathy's New York call, and when they had come roaring in, I had passed them going out. They had noticed me but they hadn't known they wanted me, not then. They talked to Cathy, but they got nowhere with her. She had pulled out of her faint all on her own and she stone-walled it with the doctor the hotel sent up. She also stone-walled it with the police.

They did better at the hotel desk. Down there they knew that Mr. Hugh Martin had never arrived to pick up his reservation even though it had been made by telephone from Siracusa the morning of that same day. They also knew that Mr. Erridge had left the hotel in a great hurry and he had left in his Porsche. Color, license number, all details.

So fuzz all over the island had been watching for Erridge, not to pick him up but to follow him; and fuzz had been alerted to muster in the area where the Rolls had last been seen. Nobody had spotted Erridge but one cop watching from that one house in the little town where I had seen the lighted window. He'd had no means for following. When the reinforcements came in, they moved toward the house.

I had to figure out the rest of it for myself, but it wasn't too hard. Vittorio had ripped the jewelry off the dying woman in Agrigento and Jack had thought it great. When he learned that it was not so great and that Vittorio had ripped off the fakes when the real thing had been there for the taking, disappointment had put him into a murderous rage, and he'd shot Vittorio.

Being a man who wouldn't waste anything, he then had

been forced to speed up the whole action. He cut the ears
off Vittorio's body and put them on ice. Like everyone
else in the world, he knew about the Getty kidnapping. For
doing an imitation of that job, the ears were going to be
useful, but they had to be used, however, while they were
still fresh. He couldn't wait till Cathy had failed to meet his
deadline before he sent her the first one, and he couldn't let
her have it for more than the first shocking sight of it because, if anyone stopped to examine it, he could come
around to recognizing that this was a bigger ear and one of
different shape, not much like the neat jobs Huddles wore
on the sides of his head. She was to have a look at one ear,
and if that didn't speed her up, it would be a look at two of
them.

It was also not too hard to understand Ercole. He hadn't
been as crazy as he seemed. He had a dead brother who,
come Judgment Day when Vittorio would come out of his
grave and pull himself together for the judging, would have
a bad time finding his ears. Ercole hadn't had any per-
verted thing for ears. He had just wanted to fix it so that
murdered Vittorio could repossess his.

While the fuzz were filling me in on the part they had
played, their head man came up with something that had
me baffled.

"There was no need, Signor Erridge, for you to avoid
us," he said, "and there was no need for the beautiful Signorina Martin to lie to us. We are Italians. We are *simpa-
tici*. In colder countries you might have reason to be afraid
that the police will interfere, but in kidnappings here in
Italy it is only the family that decides. We act only if the
family wants us to."

"And you couldn't see that Miss Martin didn't want you
to act. She didn't call you. When you came, she lied to you.
How did you understand that?"

G 44

"We understood it that she wanted us to keep hands off."

"So you went in shooting?"

"But not for the kidnapping, Signor Erridge. For the robbery. These men robbed the dead and the dying. Could we have that?"

Italian logic, Charlie. Only in Italy.

The next day Cathy was still counting Huddles' ears and kissing him and kissing me—that went on all morning—and it was still going on when Uncle Jimmie came flying in. He was as I'd expected he would be. It was impossible to tell whether he was more pleased because Huddles had been able to keep his ears or because it had become necessary for him to advance the Martins out of his own funds enough to bring the available cash up to the three-million mark.

He was scooping them up and taking them to Sardinia where, in his words, they would be "among their own kind." Nobody had to tell Erridge that he wasn't their kind, but Erridge did have to tell Cathy.

"You're coming with us," she said.

"Can't do it, Baby. If I don't get back to work and soon, I'll be hurting for bread."

"You don't ever have to work again. You know I'm rich, much, much too rich."

"That's you Cathy. It isn't me, and anyhow there are things I have to do here."

There were. I gave Vittorio and Ercole a great joint funeral even though there was nobody but me to follow the plumed horses and the hearse. I was there and I saw to it that Vittorio was buried with his ears. Ercole had wanted it that way.